HOW TO BUILD YOUR OWN DUPLEX
WITHIN MONTHS ON YOUR PRESENT INCOME

4 Great ways to achieve your goal in record of time!

ADERONMUN OLABISI ALABI

HOW TO BUILD
YOUR OWN DUPLEX
WITHIN MONTHS ON YOUR PRESENT INCOME.

HOW TO BUILD

YOUR OWN DUPLEX

WITHIN MONTHS ON YOUR PRESENT INCOME.

Aderonmun Olabisi Alabi

Contents

INTRODUCTION

This book is as inspirational as it sounds and is hopefully going to form the kernel inside that you need to make the necessary decision to build your own house. The book contains practical steps and aids after each chapter and module that the reader can do, which gradually builds up to actualizing your home dream.

It can be rather empowering to own your own property and live in it, especially in a country like ours with no real social supports. Forget rent control – it has never worked in Nigeria and the truth is, it will never work. The principle is faulty and government cannot control what it does not have. The various landlords did not purchase their property through government processes but most or all of them acquired property by private means and tend to insist on the rent that is acceptable to them in a free market economy. So there is a free flow of rent increase rather often; some occur yearly. The ordinary man caught in this cycle and the rising cost of living is faced with the daunting challenge of trying to build a house where there appears to be no funds available for this purpose.

This material will help whoever applies the principles. There has never been a time more appropriate to build your own home especially now as government has been encouraging private hands in property development and declining to build public housing.

I shared this title with a friend of mine, an insurance executive in Lagos who smiled broadly. She rented a flat six years ago and the moment she was moving into the property she gave herself a simple achievable goal that in five years from that time she wants to buy her own property and live in it. At the time she was sharing this with me, she had moved into her own property. What gave her the impetus was the kernel that she had formed inside, as determination to do it. She had given herself a five year quit notice, to leave a rented apartment and enter her own property and was excited at the possibility to turning this into a book. The very idea is to beat the landlord to it anyway, by giving yourself a notice to quit before the landlord does because he will, sooner or later.

In my career, I have seen all sort of tenancy situation that bemuse. A tenant was given a notice to quit for no reason whosoever after ten years of living in a wing of duplex. Concerned, he approached the owner of the property and asked what he had done wrong. He had been the ideal tenant for ten years paying rent promptly and living responsibly with his family. The landlord assured him it was nothing personal. He said *"No tenant stays more than 10 years in my house so that he will not think of taking over the ownership of my property. I therefore give a notice to quit to whoever has been my tenant for ten years so he or she can move on."* A crude and laughable proposition but it proves that sooner than later the landlord may ask you to move. So why not give yourself that notice before he does and achieve life's necessity.

Of course, it is not all possible for the tenant to take over ownership of the property. This could only happen if

A serious part of the process of building your own home is to accept that your present accommodation which is rented does not belong to you and you can be asked to leave whenever you cannot meet up a demand for rent increase.

there was a sale of the property as he (the tenant) bought but that was the old man's thinking. Presently this tenant is about completing his own five bedroom detached house in a government reservation area – a feat he achieved within three years of pressured, focused spending. The Notice to

Quit triggered off an internal response in him to stop moving from house to house as a tenant and finally do something for himself and he succeeded. Most people can succeed of they think, and the sure way is to set a target date or year you desire to have built your house beyond which you know you are overstaying in rented space.

A serious part of the process of building your own home is to accept that your present accommodation which is rented does not belong to you and you can be asked to leave whenever you cannot meet up a demand for rent increase. As a tenant you have confronted this thought and you know that this could happen sooner or later. You also wish you could own your own property but know that it cost millions to become a house owner which you do not necessarily possess now.

Indeed, you hope for a lumpsum miracle in the near future like hitting a lotto jackpot or winning "who wants to be a millionaire" or more realistically getting a fantastic job offer with a huge package and then presto your house is bought! Slow down, you day dreamer, -not many people ever achieve much this way. Home ownership is made possible with a saving habit which you are better off starting now. It is a process and so it could take sometime; actually just a few months (for instance maximum of 48 months) if you apply your little resources consistently.

So what do you do? First, stretch your imagination and give yourself a realistic "Notice To Quit" rented accommodation based on the number of years you envisage that your own house can be put together, judging by your income presently. Commit yourself to the singular focus of applying your savings to building your house over a period of time. The effect is delayed or postponed enjoyment of things you desire (they are often not bare necessities – they are luxuries). You can indulge in these things after achieving your immediate goal of home ownership.

Why not play this simple game by filling the form overleaf – your own Quite Notice, exclusively designed by you and for you!

GIVE

YOURSELF

A QUIT NOTICE!

GIVE YOURSELF A QUIT NOTICE

TROJAN

SOLICITORS

People's Well-Being Chambers

No. 1 My Own House Way Tenants Ville

_______________________)

_______________________) Fill in your name and address

_______________________)

Dear Sir/Madam,

RE: TENANCY OF (FLAT, DUPLEX, HOUSE) AT

____

____

____

____

____

____

(Fill in your current address which you hope to leave to your

own self actualized apartment)

We   Act   as   Solicitors   to

_________________________________ (your own name,

not your landlord!!) and have his instructions to give you a

_________________ (months/years).

Notice to Quit the above stated addressed which you presently occupy (**Note:** *The notice period does not have to comply with any statutory or legal provisions – just how long you realistically envisage you need to pool resource together to build or buy your own and move).*

We are constrained to do this because our client wants you to vacate the premises for clear purpose as state –

i.   To avoid continuous landlord/agents harassment on rent increase.

ii. To reduce conflict between tenants in the block and all the cat parking problems

iii. To get a better life and leave the substandard house you live in presently.

iv. To change area for better services and utilities and live well

v.   To avoid the everyday anxiety of living a rented apartment.

vi.   To fulfill one of life's simple goals!

vii.   In fact to leave because of the mosquitoes in this area
        that always go through these nets anyway!

viii.   To give my wife and children better quality lives!

Please be careful to work towards leaving by the above date and yielding up possession. Any period overstayed will be calculated against your goodself and cost you *mesne profits.*

We will not hesitate to commence and action against you in the court of law if we observed that your attitude is unserious!

Please be warned!

Dated this _______ day of ___________________ 20 ___________

                                        Yours faithfully,

                                        For: **Trojan Chambers**

Note: This Notice of Quit is issued to you to yourself and as simple as it looks, it is the initial seed you need to actually work at something fairly easy to achieve. Few thing are more powerful than writing down your vision or

goals and so believe that in time you have set, real progress will be made. What if you have not finished the house by that date? Do not even entertain such thoughts now – it is much too early. Focus on the immediate first steps you must take towards building your own house and getting out of rented space fast!

For once do not handle this issue lightly. It is one of life's most empowering moves that can set you and your family free!
Enjoy your study.

MODULE ONE

It's Your Life!

There is such great diversity in the way people are formed and moulded in life. Predictably, the way people turn out is equally different. As a result, we will carry out the business of daily living with various objectives, focus, attitudes and temperaments. Somewhere in between, every forward looking person wants to succeed. This is the desire that drives us to carry on at work, at home and all other involvements.

Success means different things to different people but one of the common denominators of measuring success is the degree to which personal comfort is attained; the possession of a home, car(s) and enough money and resources to sustain one's desirable lifestyle. Not enough people ever attain these heights when compared to the teeming population but quite a lot of folks try hard to build at least one house in their lifetime

TYPE 1 PROFILE

Attaining home ownership to many is an awesome task. The sheer thought of the amount of investment to carry it through is daunting and causes many people to keep pushing it forward until a later date. Inevitably by this arrangement, the issue of owning a house is postponed for a time they perceive should be easier.

For such people amounts that came their way that could be saved after meeting their bare necessities are usually committed to "small" pleasures that makes life feel good and worth living. Their housing consumption is still in the form of rents which take a chunk of their disposable income (see the book, *How to Deal with Shylock Landlord*) and most of such people never even as much as buy a plot of land in anticipation of building soon. Somewhere in their mind, it is really just a wish.

There are others who take the issue of personal housing very seriously. Coming from a humble background such a person may waste no time at all buying a plot of land as soon as he can put some savings together. Many go ahead to buy a plot in whichever located as long as their savings can cover the cost of land – *a situation of cutting your coat according to your cloth! Not your size!* Such groups of people are usually related to *uncle scrooge* the comic character who scrounges and saves up every bit and penny.

They mould sandcrete blocks themselves on site instead of patronizing a block factory in an effort to save some money. They wait to buy cement at control price from a friend a relation who is either a distributor a cement factory worker and do all kinds of cost cutting gymnastic. Of course such people source direct cheap labour and once their present level of savings is exhausted they stop only to commence again when a little more money is available.

Eventually, some people succeed in putting a house together in this way even if it does not meet the international definition of qualitative housing. It passes as a roof over their head. Unfortunately due to other pressing needs for money like school fees, feeding and vehicle maintenance there are others in this category who get stuck midway in building a house and end up for years with uncompleted houses.

TYPE 3 PROFILE

Far too many people in this last category end up with regrets. People who could easily afford to build or buy their own house just by giving it some attention. It is easy for real estate practitioner viz an estate surveyor and valuer to observe this cross section of people due to personal interaction with people demanding housing.

A middle-aged man once turned up to inspect a number of residential properties with a view to commencing a tenancy. He wanted to leave a flat he had occupied for six years for a more spacious house. After several inspections he finally summed up regrettably that he could not afford any of the bigger accommodation he had just viewed.

He lamented that when he should have built a house of his own, he wasted his resources in high living spending on things that had no lasting value. He confessed that the only thing that reminds him of the sort of wealth he once had was a wristwatch that he bought years back in the United State of America which cost him a whopping $10,000. For him it was such a painful reminder of his past mistake because at the present time he did not have much left to pay for rented accommodation when only a few years back he could have paid for his own house with just a little bit of focus and financial discipline.

Some other person may exclaim, "Well I have never had such money before. If I have it, I won't waste the opportunity!" it is not true. It is not about the amount of money but individual attitudes to handling money. Several people may be exposed to much smaller sums and yet waste it on high living. It may be interesting to note that it is these supposedly small sums that are useful to actualize yourself build effort.

Another young man also confessed to and odd craving he used to spend money on. He occupied a modest two bedroom flat that was sparsely furnished and worked as a self-employed engineer. Soon he started making some money part of which he could have saved but he would leave his apartment every weekend and check into a five star hotel in the same city where he lived and had his flat. After spending two or three nights of sheer luxury ordering room service he would return to his poorly furnished flat. Soon there was a downturn in his work and he began to have regrets about the way the handle his savings before. It saddened him that he never thought of buying a plot of land or even furnishing his small flat to taste when the going was good.

Have you noticed that both persons in these two examples only reviewed their lives with the benefit of hindsight? Not when the going was good. It goes to show that many more people are right now wasting similar opportunities and may later have regrets. The lesson ought to be that once you have resources, one of the greatest priorities you should have is to channel it to building for yourself. Each of the above profiles have a lot to improve and build upon with the information contained in this book.

Ultimately, its your life!

TAKE A NEW LOOK AT YOUR INCOME

To really benefit from this book and actually build your own apartment you must have an income. In simple terms, your income is your earnings from your business or vocation. If you can properly grasp this part you can succeed at building your first house in a short time because the keys lies with how you interpret your earnings. So many people earn a lot of money and yet fail to account for how it is spent at the end of the day.

At a seminar, a young banker looking rather worried came up to ask for advice. "Sir, I earn a total package of N2.4 million yearly and somehow I can't explain why I still don't have my assets" He then attempted to throw more light. "I'm the first born in my family and my siblings are always on my case with one request or the other and all my friends pester me for phone cards and I end up trying to satisfy everybody." Somehow this young man and perhaps everyone in the similar problems of controlled spending knows the areas of leakages that make their income not amount to much but are unable to come out with a fair analysis and line of action. If you x-ray your income and streamline your spending, you are simply developing financial intelligence. In other words, it is possible for the young banker to keep helping his siblings and still save some money systematically to begin the acquisition of assets.

There are other workers who are also salary earners and don't earn this sort of money stated above. They also must apply these principles and maximize their resources to build. We must commence on some basic principles of economics here. Income is abbreviated as

(i) When you receive your earnings, it is either you spend all or part which is termed as consumption – C or save some part which is termed S.

$$\text{Therefore Income} = \text{Consumption} + \text{Savings}$$

$$I = C + S$$

<table>
<tr><td>

If you x-ray your income and streamline your spending, you are simply developing financial intelligence.

</td></tr>
</table>

Think about it, when you earn money, you spend some part of it on your needs and requirements (consumption). There effort made to keep some aside for the rainy day results in savings. But these days it is possible for income to equal consumption (I=C) leaving nothing for savings. The pressure for rising living expenses is much. This is the truth about people in many nations of the world including the United States of America. Most people spend all their income and still go on to incur huge credit card debts. What this means is that people are either spending all their income on bills and purchases or

worse still, spending money they have not earned and going into debt.

Handling money appears to be quite some challenge. First is the issue of the young banker who can't really save

money. He also does not apply financial intelligence because he has no systematic way of deploying his earnings to increase wealth and he feels or knows, like many other people in similar situations, that he isn't getting it right yet.

Next is the proposition that after monthly expenses have been deducted from your income, real effort should be made to save money on a consistent basis. It is the ability to save some part of your income that makes it possible to apply such savings for other uses.

Do you have enough intelligence to organize your spending so that priorities come first? Are the things you prioritize really priorities? Can you cut down on telephone expenses? Can you reduce the number of shirts and cuff-links you just bought from six to three? Can you reduce visits to restaurants, bars and fast foods joints? Increase your home cooked meals.

Consciously, determine what amount of your income you should give away monthly. Once you have given that amount out fully this month, the rest may have to wait till next month. The ability to pull yourself out of the consumption habit and create savings is the sure way of getting into home ownership. Remember, it is not about the amount you earn because this savings principle applies to both high and low income earners.

SOME FOLKS JUST CAN'T SAVE!

Lastly to introduce some balance, the reality is that many people try to save money from their income but it just isn't possible. Such people who are usually more in the low income bracket and small traders in the informal sector of the economy may find that they cannot meet their basic monthly bills. Their total income is shared between transport fares to work daily, feeding costs of the family, paying rent (even for a single room apartment) and finally, coping with school fees.

In a developed country this group would surely benefit from government's social housing provision. In the third world countries however, this is not usually the case and yet a lot of people keep hoping for this mirage of a "better life".

If you are in this category and find you cannot save up from your income for any landed property purchase, it is easy to "give up" on the inside of you and find something to blame it on – Government? You family? God? A close friend? Justified as you may be, this position does not really change anything. Rather, what can be practically done is to motivate yourself into the next rung on the ladder by doing something to improve your income earning. **Look for a new job; acquire a new skill or qualification; start a newer fast moving product.** All these may not happen overnight but let your days be spent usefully making improvements. Many people will eventually improve income and this consequently makes it possible to save money.

Remember, the ability to save depends on your income level and the extent of needs you have to meet, which is relative. It will vary in many individual circumstances but let each person work something out that works or else this one life is not getting much done. Also remember, save needs to be applied to increase your wealth and assets. Saving is not an end in itself. In other words, you can be a great money saver and still end up poor and homeless. Convert your savings early into enduring assets chief of which is your home. Nothing ventured, nothing gained.

APPRECIATING ASSETS OR DEPRECIATING/WASTING ASSETS?

What is it that people are acquiring with their savings anyway? This is a legitimate question that everyone should reflect upon. Do not pass the buck – take yourself up on the issue of how you spend your savings! Chances are that a closer look at the things you buy or pay for (without being prejudice) can help to re-align your finances and release the sort of funds you need to channel towards your own house. This move automatically blocks off the avenues of waste and leakage.

Below is a fairly detailed list of common assets that people generally spend money on. Some of them are immovable assets like a plot of land or block of flats and the others are chattels or moveable property. All of them are important and good to have and depending on individual preferences everyone chooses which on is most pressing to have now and then take money out of the bank to pay for them.

Immovable property which is rightly termed real estate or landed property is described as an **appreciating asset.** This is because progressively over time its value keeps going up. Even when inflation is high its value still goes higher and those who are knowledgeable use this as a way of keeping or preserving their wealth since they can get much higher value for such assets in the market than what was originally paid for it.

All the others are called **depreciating or wasting assets.** Accountants are quits conversant with this term as well as estate surveyors and valuers. The idea is that these assets decline gradually in value from the moment they are bought over a relative period of time.

The effect is that you can only get a residual value much lower than the cost price if you decide to sell after a few months or years. It is common news that as valuable as a brand new car is, the moment it is bought and driven out of the showroom it begins to loose value. A mobile phone also looses value after a few months of the rave it creates no matter how beautiful it may be, especially when a trendier phone is released into the market.

This is why smart alecs spend good money on appreciating assets and less money on the equally to increase your wealth and assets. Saving is not an end in itself. In other words, you can be a great money saver and still end up poor and homeless. Convert your savings early into enduring assets chief of which is your home. Nothing ventured, nothing gained.

APPRECIATING ASSETS OR DEPRECIATING / WASTING ASSETS?

What is it that people are acquiring with their savings anyway? This is a legitimate question that everyone should reflect upon. Do not pass the buck – take yourself up on the issue of how you spend your savings! Chances are that a closer look at the things you buy or pay for (without being prejudice) can help to re-align your finances and release the sort of funds you need to channel towards your own house. This move automatically blocks off the avenues of waste and leakage.

Below is a fairly detailed list of common assets that people generally spend money on. Some of them are immovable assets like a plot of land or block of flats and the others are chattels or moveable property. All of them are important and good to have and depending on individual preferences everyone chooses which one is most pressing to have now and then take money out of the bank to pay for them.

Immovable property which is rightly termed real estate or land property is described as an **appreciating assets.** This is because progressively over time its value still goes higher and those who are knowledgeable use this as a way of keeping or preserving their wealth since they can get much higher value for such assets in the market than that what was originally paid for it.

All the others are called **depreciating or wasting assets**. Accountants are quite conversant with this term as well as estate surveyors and valuers. The idea is that these assets decline gradually in value from the moment they are bought over a relative period of time.

The effect is that you can only get a residual value much lower than the cost price if you decide to sell after a few months or years. It is common news that as valuable as a brand new car is, the moment it is bought and driven out of the showroom it begins to loose value. A mobile phone also looses value after a few months of the rave it creates no matter how beautiful it may be, especially when a trendier phone is released into the market.

This is why smart alecs spend good money on appreciating assets and less money on the equally essential depreciating assets. Actually, the moment you hear the term wasting assets something should stir inside you to avoid wasting resources. The arduous task of the accountant really is to determine the rate that will be applied to depreciate or cut down the value of depreciating assets.

Home appliances – latest TV, electronic gadgets, Hi-fi etc	• Depreciating assets.
Jewelry, Clothes, Swiss voile	• Depreciating assets.
Fleet of Cars – many times more than the value of a house in cost	• Depreciating assets.
Expensive Parties	?...

Frequent pleasure trips abroad	?..
Extra marital affairs	?..
GSM phones (state of the art) and Phone cards (for girl friends too!)	?..
Marry more wives	?..
Chieftaincy titles	?..
Plot of land	• Appreciating assets
Purchase of a building	• Appreciating assets
Stock and Shares	• Appreciating assets

The above is fairly representative of what people spend their money upon. Sometimes, some have unknowingly spent money on some of these items much more than is required to finish a whole house!

All that is advised is to re-order these priorities to make the need for housing possible.

DON'T JUST KEEP CASH

There is also a sensible argument against keeping money idle in your bank account as you save. Cash savings will only earn for you a small amount which the bank pays as interest. If money is kept in the bank for too long, inflation occurring on the outside (within the economy) tends to eat up too much of its value and this is not good for the saver.

Say for instance, a bag of cement sold for N500.00 (five hundred naira) a year ago when you started saving up and currently sells for N850.00 (eight hundred and fifty naira) only; it means there has been a 70% increase in the price of cement (or other products0. Based on going bank interest rates you have been paid 14% on your amount saved. Your savings can no longer buy the number of cement bags you could have bought a year ago. We are in an inflationary economy and it is best to use up money in building before long, or invest it in the interim, in sage investment that yield quick returns like the stock market. Alternatively, simply buy plots of land (all these will be treated in greater detail later on).

ACTION PLAN

    A. Carry out this simple exercise

    Identify your source(s) of income

Employment

Monthly salary | Annual contract | Temp/replacement or relief staff | Casual worker | Commission earnings Highly paid, highly skilled workers.

Self Employed

| Professional | Fee based earnings | Professional – receive payment for services |

|Professional | Engaged as a consultant in an institution/organization

Self Employed [Informal Sector]

|Artisans – carpenter, plumber, bricklayer, electrician, gardener, clear

| Pretty/small trader – market women, GSM shops, street hawkers, roadside food sellers

| Small service companies – lift/mechanical/industrial plumbing service.

Business Owners

| Trading companies | Distributors of products/services | Chemists | Importers & Exporters | Organised/mechanical farming | Printing & Publishing |Real Estate investors & developers | Commercial banking | Mortgage banking | Merchant banking | Insurance Companies | Haulage companies | Security services | Building and civil engineering companies | General contractors/Suppliers | Fast food chains | Franchisees/Manufacturer's Representative | Department stores | Boutiques.

Investors

| Substantial investments in real estate – commercial, industrial, residential and institutional (including private secondary schools and universities)

| Large investment in stocks and shares of quoted companies at the Stock Exchange |

These are not exhaustive but are designed to help the sorting process. Each person can immediately appreciate where their income comes from. Since the source of our income flow differs, it may affect the way each individual saves.

Conversely, it almost surely affects the way individuals spend. An engineering consultant who has just been paid N12 million for designing three bridges and a 120 kilometre stretch of dual carriage road can easily decide to purchase a new car costing N5 million. He simply postulates that jobs of this nature will keep coming into his practice. Another engineer earning a monthly salary of N500,000 and a total package of N8.4 million per annum (plus allowances) may not be able to expend money in the same way because he has other monthly expenses to cope with and cannot deduct this lumpsum.

Each person from this can analyse their income their income and devise a saving plan.

Sometimes people have more than one source of income.

- **They are able to operate both as employed and self employed,** for instance, some university lecturers who still open offices to practice their profession.

- **they are Moonshiners** – people who close at 5pm and proceed to their own shop or office until nightfall and earn another stream of income.

- **They are Rent seekers** – usually applies to government officials or political appointees who earn additional sums other than their pay by corrupt means.

- **They earn occasional windfalls** – due to knowing a highly placed person for a season or by some peculiar circumstance you can to execute some jobs that gave substantial returns that are significant.

DEVISE A SAVING PLAN YOU CAN KEEP TO

The reason for this exercise so far is not for a feel good ego trip. It is intended to help you organize your thought process to appreciate how much income gets into your hands. By this overview you can then say to yourself – save at least 30% - 50% of your income yearly depending on who you are and your financial responsibilities. Some others could simply decide that at least 50% for every windfall must go into savings (This applies most to contract jobs and professional fees).

In clear terms the nature of your earnings will determine your savings plan. Your own personal propensity to save determines how far you want to go with saving. Unless you cultivate the discipline you will not save or you may save and jeep withdrawing money for other things at the slightest pressure. Which way forward?

1. How much do you spend per month? ▢

    (Feeding, transport, vehicles maintenance, fuel, give away etc)

2. Locate and itemize expenses occurring en-bloc at different times of the year ▢
    (school fees, parents support, holiday cost, medical check-ups, etc)

3. What is your current level of saving after expenses

    | % | NIL |

4. If NIL, is your income likely to grow in your present vocation?

5. If NIL, are there items on your expenses list you can cut down or ▢
    remove temporarily to make saving possible?

6. If yes, indicate them below

a. ____

   ____

b. ____

   ____

c. ____

   ____

d. ____

   ____

7. Do you have another source of income?

    -   Occasional jobs/contract   ☐

    -   Moon lighting (working afterhours)   ☐

    -   Others   ☐

8. How do you spend your "extra" income?   ☐

9. Based on your expenses list in (1) and (2) can you streamline and save

    more money from your other sources?

    ☐

10. Now roughly calculate how much you can save yearly?

<table><tr><td>

</td></tr><tr><td>
</td></tr></table>

11. How best can you keep your saving without spending it?

The underlisted are the common ways:

- Term/Fixed Deposit
- Saving Account (with passbook – the old way!)
- Target savings:
  - Cooperative – *Ajo*
  - *Esusu,* micro-credit
  - Bank target saving
- Compulsory/regular purchase of shares and stock
- Land purchase (ensure that you are well informed about this option to avoid losses in land transactions).

The best way to keep the savings you truly want to apply for your building construction is to keep it in a form that you cannot easily reach. Some can buy shares and discover that the effort to sell is not easy. These people will not call their broker at every frivolous reason (Good!). Others will engage in good cooperative target savings and the last to collect the takings. Be sincere enough to pick a method that works.

Lastly, stick to the habit you have just evolved and every time you are tempted to give up, consider the timeframe you have given yourself to quit rented accommodation. Then work at it! **Don't give up.**

MODULE TWO
GETTING STARTED

Depending on your attitude, so far if you have gone through the preceding chapters and followed the Action Plan, you are on the sure path to achieving home ownership. There is always something about starting a

It is usual to fight thoughts that want you to procrastinate until a future date when you should be more comfortable but the secret and way forward is to get started!

new journey. You may experience some anxiety or mixed feeling about whether you meager savings can actually start and finish the building effort. It is alright to toss up and down your bed in deep thought. It is usual to fight thoughts that want you to procrastinate until a future date when you should be more comfortable but the secret and way forward is to get started!

One you have bought a plot of land you can build (Truth #1). There are a number of processes that you need to go through quickly before starting your building foundation (Truth #2). Once you get past the processes the first thing that you do is **setting out** (those wooden pegs and strings put in place before the foundation trenches are dug) and then the **foundation.** Remember those days when the older folks used to do foundation laying ceremonies? Anyway you can skip all that nowadays. The vital thing is to accomplish this first feat of property, building the foundation (substructure).

Later on the book, the ways to find responsible builders will be highlighted. Some people cannot stand building and others don't have the time to oversee things themselves. There are ways to get round each challenge as long as you are willing. Is building a risk? Not really. Is starting a building without having all the money really a risk? No! Not as risky as starting a business or a trade. In any case when you attend business seminars and the issue of risks comes up you are often encouraged to take risks! They say "Life itself is a risk!" most people who have succeeded at self-build efforts did not have all the money ready. Even where you have substantial sums that can complete the house, finish costs towards the end of completion and inflation will still upset cost projections. The best thing therefore is to start and follow a stage by stage progression.

ULTIMATELY YOU CAN LIVE
WHEREVER YOU WANT!

Perhaps you are one of those people that refuse to start anything at all because you cannot afford to buy a house or plot in your preferred neighbourhood or the sort of area(s) where your friends live. It is a common conflict but the bitter truth is that for every year you refuse to get started, you may just be a little further away from your home dream.

Why is this so? A well located plot of land in Lekki Phase 1 in 2001 cost between N2.5m to N4m. Presently in 2005 the same plot cost a range between N12m to N22m or more – no value added – just bare sites. Now if you could not afford it at your level in 2001, it is a bit more difficult now because prices have skyrocketed but your earnings or savings have not.

Some people are speaking out loud – "Miracles of a windfall still happen!" Yes it is true, but it is not absolute wisdom to predicate life's important goals on the premise of a coming business windfall which may never come. It is better to start doing something now even if it is not exactly your best choice or location. In Robert Kiyosaki's Rich Dad, Poor Dad, rich dad was a smart investor who attained financial independence and could afford a lot of life's pleasures and luxuries. His investments began to pay for his lifestyle. Poor Dad on the other hand remained a hardworking, honest and sincere person earning a regular income but never climbing up the investment ladder. It is all about dreams, choices and information.

In the other series of Marvtechservice "How to" books there is emphasis on the principle that real estate is an investment. Every time you purchase landed property whether a bare site or even your personal home, it is an investment that yields returns. Your home can yield capital increases or an annual income (rents). Your personal occupation of the house is really an opportunity cost. As long as you remember this, you will realize that putting money into any landed property is an investment for the future. You will always have the option of holding your property or selling it for returns or capital gains as long as there is a property market. Hold onto this principle because it is amplified now and elsewhere in this book.

A young business owner servicing some of the fast food chain in Lagos recently completed his twin duplexes in Lekki Phase 1. He occupied one wing and offered the other wing for rent. His move as well thought out because he actually had the option of building a detached house that would stand alone. He could choose to live without the interference of a tenant in the next wing but he decided that the N1.5 million income that would come in annually was worth the bother (now that is smart thinking). A year after moving into his new apartment he told a couple of friends that he hoped to spend just five years in his new house. Within this time he hopes to move to Banana Island! Lagos.

What nerve? Yet a lot of people are accomplishing similar goals in different parts of the country all the time. Most of the time those who move up to better locations like the above young man, may just be living their lives normally and build in the first place they can afford. Gradually as their fortunes change and they save up more they take up the next opportunity and move up higher.

Therefore keep your eyes on your choice location but invest now in the level that your substantial savings can take you. That is the station of life in which you find yourself presently. If your ultimate location is Ajah but you can afford to get a property in Ogba, Ikeja in the interim, go ahead and invest in Ikeja. Ajah is only worth holding on for if by your current savings or investment level you can realistically accomplish your Ajah home next year or the year after. Otherwise take it in your stride – enjoy this level and like the other young man anticipate with great hope and focus the next level.

There is not stereotype as to how it can be achieved but cumulatively, if it is your passion you will soon have multiple investments in all these average locations since you have wasted no opportunity. All your savings, you have for several years, converted to real estate. Three average properties in Ikeja can all pay for your Lagos Island dream if sold. You may retain one property for rental income and future price gain in Ikeja, dispose of two others and see your new house in Ajah through together with your new savings. The options are several once you have attained multiple ownership.

This just proves that once you are in tune with real estate investment habits, the options are wide open and your resources are broader. Much better than if you waited for years in the same coach hoping for that ideal location. But now over the years, you have changed coaches, you have changed stations and your present station in life has brought you from the rear. From third class, you now ride in a first class coach! What an adventure!

Think 3-dimensionally:
Imagine Your House!

By now you are probably wondering whether you bought a book relating to the power of positive thinking. No. However, like many serious endeavours, if you can achieve accurate details by careful planning and thought processes the active part that deals with actual building construction becomes easy.

Not everyone can imagine in 3-dimension, that is, view images in your mind's eye from all its sides and angles. Mostly, photographs are presented in 2-dimensions. This is why some clients ask their architect to create a model (a miniature of what the house will really look like reduced to scale) in order to be able to appreciate the final product.

The importance of imaging your house is to actually be able to have your own input in the house, just the way you want it. Details like the kitchen size, the bathroom size and position or orientation relative to other parts of the house can be influenced by you. Unless it is absolutely ill-advised, the architect is interested in his client's brief and will follow your wishes. But some people just tell the architect to draw something and it is only when the building is up that they start seeing that the kitchen is too small, the wardrobe space is adequate and the house is designed to have three different levels. All to their dismay.

Benefits of this exercise include the underlisted:

- **YOU CAN HAVE A GRASP ON THE ACTUAL SIZE OF THE HOUSE.** If the design is bigger than you planned, it can have serious cost implications. If the design is small the house may not meet your family's requirements.

- **YOU CAN INPUT ENOUGH FACILITIES** like the number of sockets (single or double) in the sitting area, the bedrooms, the taps/faucets, the plumbing system, conduit TV and intercom wiring and so on. Little things that make all the difference and add convenience to your home living.

- **YOU CAN PREPARE THE GROUNDS FOR THE TYPE OF FINISHES YOU WANT IN YOURSELF –** the flooring, the ceiling, the roof covering, window and door types (make a list of these if you want).

- **IT IS BETTER TO GET INVOLVED AT THIS STAGE AND ANTICIPATE WHAT YOU ARE TRYING TO BUILD.** Never mind if you see new things along the way and want to change something. It is always possible to alter and manipulate the building details, even while construction is going on.

Study The Direction Of City Growth:

Arteries Of Development

This is another clever tip in the pursuit of home ownership. Like elimination series, as you worry about what your house should look like and the internal arrangement, at least worry about where you will locate the house as well! Actually everybody has a good idea of where they desire house to be as earlier stated. At least until they finally go out of their way to contact an estate agent and find out how much a plot of land is sold for in their preferred location. The asking price of the plot is usually way too high to afford in their area of first choice.

The next challenge is to find an acceptable alternative location that fits the amount of money saved up for a plot of land. At this point it is not unusual to turn up with several alternatives, none of which is wholly acceptable like the first choice. After several inspections with estate agents to various neighbourhoods (average areas of comparable level) that fit your price range you are still left with the challenge of making a good choice.

Using the Abuja example, let us imagine that someone set out to build his residence in Garki Village or Wuse Zone 6 but discovers he cannot afford the price of plots in either of the two areas. He has been offered alternative plots in Apo, Kado, Jabi, Gwarinpa and Lugbe.

The way Abuja, Nigeria's capital city has evolved, this person's choice areas fall within the original planned city, bet he cannot afford it. The alternative five neighbourhoods he has been offered are scattered in different parts of the outskirts of the city in different directions. These fit his purse but he is confronted with the problem of choosing one of five alternatives.

Eventually the way forward for such a person is to weigh each area by its obvious advantages and disadvantages and then select the one that best fits the real choice you could afford. What is it you don't like about each of these five areas? Which once can you live with? Its all cognitive and it only takes a brief mental process and your choice is made.

Like Abuja, virtually every town or city in Nigeria is daily evolving a pattern of development and growth that leaves the centre congested and new areas springing up on the periphery or outskirts. Most of the new areas are either unplanned or lack effective planning control. This may leave the neighbourhood in a very bad shape with blighting tendencies that suggest that it will get worse. Based on other factors, some other poorly planned neighbourhood may have potentials for future improvements. The critical factor is making the right choice among these options. It can determine the future of your investment in this new home you are about to build.

Signs to look out for:

- **Does government have any plans to improve the area now or in the near future?** (Find out through the grapevine/local government offices/state government).
- **How far out of town is the area and how good is the access route?**
- **Is there any proposed government institution, estate, or facility in the area that will bring attention and development?**
- **What level of services/utilities are being provided?** Electricity, mains water and telephone.
- **Who are the predominant buyers of plots and properties in the area?** They should be people that fit into your station of life. The obvious reason is the fact that cooperation for joint communal development will be easier to achieve and afford. Such an area has a good chance with people of like mind.

- **Can you estimate obvious nuisance value?** It is minus. A really nasty traffic bottleneck before getting to the area; an uncontrolled source of noise pollution; bad erosion and drainage problems that remain untackled.

- **Proximity to an existing residential estate** that is well planned.

By diligently doing this exercise, you are consciously making the best of your home investment. A careless choice without enough of these considerations may cause your new house to stick out of the area like a sore thumb. Later regrets can be avoided from the onset. This is why some people ultimately don't mind their plot costing more than the house! Although you cannot afford your ultimate location now, make the best of the choice before you!

This analysis of the direction of city growth also holds the key to where to buy multiple plots, should you decide to hold your savings by investing in several plots.

Buy A Piece Of Land From Your Savings Every Year

It is alright to quickly reel back and try to ensure yourself that you are actually following the core principles

that you are being loaded with in this book. What a huge cocktail of all sorts of things mixed together. When you practice these things and acquire the dexterity to make it all work together, you attain such a good blend you would hardly believe the results. It is such people that eventually look back and are almost amused at how easy it now appears after their first home and may be, several other home are standing.

This cocktail of all the "right moves" that make your home dream possible is both an art and a science. Some people would say they have a knack for building and putting things together. They further admit that they just toy with few ideas and apply some little money to get the results that we see. All these things are just the result of real estate investment habits created by each individual in his or her own little world. With some focus and simple adherence, results are produced.

There is this simple wealth creating principle quite a lot of people can practice. But a plot of land every year from your savings. In the introductory portion of this book, we viewed the type 1 profile as someone who spends his savings on "small pleasures" as the years go by. He is however still careful to keep his gaze on home ownership – something to accomplish in some distant future. Such a person can easily buy a plot every year and in five years have five plots.

Why bother to do this?

- **Firstly, you trap your savings in a form that you cannot spend as you like.** It also comes back to you with appreciable increase. Remember, real estate is an appreciating asset and ultimately a hedge against inflation. (refer to the book *How To Make Huge Profits in Estate Agency.*)

- **Secondly, as development and city growth takes place, some areas or neighbourhoods just surprisingly transform**. Suddenly, the place is looking full of beautiful houses, roads and facilities. The early birds who bought land when it was still not attractive are the real winners. The newcomers have paid the full price for such plots because they bought when it was full blown. If your habit is to buy plots routinely, you will experience this.

- **Thirdly, land is the first see towards building a house**. You cannot build a space or suspend your house in the air, you need a plot. As you purchase several plots, even if the locations are not the sort of place you can live in, you create options for your ultimate goal. This is how it works for example. The plots you have bought in the last two years cost N200,000 each. Two years later, one is worth N350,000 and the other N400,000. If you decide to sell now (and there is always a market even though it may take a few months to dispose), cumulatively you now have N750,000. If the area you really desire cost N1million per plot you are only N250,000 away. One the other hand, one of the locations where you have your plot may speed up growth and you now have a plot in a nice area which you bought cheap!

- **Fourthly, there is a settled feeling you experience when you own a plot that is undisputed**. It's a **Can be – Can do** feeling. You have the knowing that what you actually need now is to move to site and commence foundation laying.

- **Lastly, do you know that you can actually buy up enough plots that will pay fully for the construction of your entire building?** It is real and practical. Actually if done consciously over the next four to five years it is a good way of stockpiling wealth ready to cash in and build. Simply retain one of the plots for your own use, sell all the others and return to your plot with all your arsenal (in form of money) to start building.

In conclusion, every time this principle has been shared at seminars, a consistent but legitimate question always comes up.

How do you safeguard so many plots of land against trespassers knowing that land transactions are usually fraught with problems? Well, just knowing this truth alone should make you more cautious as you approach the issue of land purchases. Refer to the book, *How To Buy Property Safely in Nigeria* for good information on how properly buy a land. There are enough tips that should help get you out of the woods. After purchasing land, either fence up and lock it or put someone on it to farm it. Make sure you remain in occupation. Later on we shall examine the cooperative principle/idea and how it can aid your land acquisitions.

ACTION PLAN

1. **Try your hands on a design or sketch of the way you want your house to look.**

   - Keep it at simple, crude floor plan. Relate the internal spaces the way you envisage. Where the sitting room would be, in relation to the bedrooms. How many toilets/baths do you want? Position the kitchen and store.

   - It is your dream, so express it. Also, your rough sketch, when shown to your architect could reveal a lot that helps in the final design.

2. **<u>Conduct a round of important exercises.</u>**

   - Drive around the city all over again, this time with the specific intention of spotting details you could not see before. You can now put to use what you have learnt about observing the direction of city growth and tell tales of knowing the quality of each new upcoming area.

- Next try to identify reputable companies that sell land in your area(s) of choice. Concentrate on looking for registered Estate Surveyors and Valuers for reasons of integrity. Those who belong as members of the Nigerian Institution of Estate Surveyors and Valuers (NIESV)

- Prepare to buy your first plot!

MODULE THREE
The Realistic House Builder

THE METHOD OF INCREMENTAL BUILDING

This method is predictably the way most people will build their own house. If an accurate survey is done and all existing house owners cooperate, at least 80-90% of accomplished home owners will accede to building incrementally. This method is simple language refers to starting a house from foundation and adding its features and structures one by one, level by level, as the builder can afford until the ultimate completed picture is achieved.

Its greater popularity lies in the truth that the building is entirely at the owner's mercy and he can take as long as his resources permit – one step at a time. Today, one thousand blocks, tomorrow iron rods, gravel, sand and cement just enough for the lintels (the concrete beams above window and doors) and every addition

> *Using incremental method of building has nothing to do with your status, a professor or bank executive can use it and messengers or clerks as well!*

lends to the greater picture of the house you will eventually live in.

The often beneficiaries of this medium of constructing houses are those who at some point experienced landlords trouble and struggle to escape the hangman's noose in a desperate effort to survive (see the book, *How To Deal With*

Shylock Landlords – A Tenant's Guide). Some of the so called landlord's palaver are perceived while some are real. This is neither an argument for or against the landlord since this is not the focus of this book but after giving accommodation problems a long thought, many people take the plunge by desperately going ahead to start building for themselves; a place devoid of anyone else's control!

Inadvertently because they do not have much resources, even as they start they commence using the incremental method. **Somehow, it is embraced and popular because it allows for flexibility and most people who are focused succeed at the level of their income.** Never mind the point at which some families move in – the house is barely completed. The plastering may be done internally leaving the exterior because there is no money yet and they just hand the external doors for security and protection from weather and move in.

Without needing to appeal to you, it is already obvious to you that your saving pattern and resources can best be applied to building using this method – **so use it and start now!** There are others, who don't have to go through much pacing with their construction. This and other ways will be highlighted in later pages but the essence is to see the most basic scenario working.

Using incremental method of building has nothing to do with your status, a professor or bank executive can use it and messengers or clerks as well! It may indeed be shocking to discover that several of the poorly paid staff in their categories have achieved home ownership! The difference is the quality of the house they are able to afford. Building incrementally does not indicate that you lower standards. This is where the issue of income, affordability and status will make the difference – **you can exploit it!**

Choose Your Style, Your Pace And Time

Obviously you are going to need professional help which will be discussed in the next pages or else you could earn some hard knocks and make mistakes in building. And boy, there is no shortage of workers in this industry – at least not yet. Try not to undermine professionals input, it can make the difference in your new project and help a great deal. The problem is that people run away from paying fees, which is cowardly. Engage professionals and let them know how much you can pay. You will surely get concession and fee cuts.

Now you have quite some latitude especially when you have good professional advisers and experienced artisans. You can choose your style once you know the different stages and levels your building will go through. Similarly you can choose your pace and the time takes to complete your house. All these tally with your earlier financial preparations as you saved up and re-ordered your spending pattern.

STYLE

Some people buy materials at every stage as it is needed and pay the bricklayer/foreman/contractor labour only; also at each stage. At foundation level, they have an agreed figure on labour that covers digging/excavation, concrete blinding, masonry or block laying and so on. This same approach is used for every other stage after the foundation is built.

Other may opt for the builders organizing to buy materials at each stage when funds are available. In other words, the builder calculates materials plus labour at every pre-agreed stage and presents his bill to you his client. There are so many other ways of approaching building work and you are free to evolve whatever works for you.

PACE

The pace really would depend ultimately on your immediate or long-term reason(s) for building a house. Again this is where individuals differ. Some people are organized enough to pace their spending on construction to give it a 4-year plan or even a 10-year plan! Some other person does not have the patience of such a long wait and wants it done and over with. This affects the pace of construction since the owner really is the driver. Some others are driven more by circumstance and need to move out of their present abode and so work faster.

TIME

Pace and time are closely related. The pace of work at each stage affects the timing of completion. These things are entirely your prerogative and you call the shots. Deep down you know your financial capacity to cope and you are cope and you are committed. The only issue with time is that builders will advise against rushing too much so that concrete can cure (giving it time to achieve enough strength). They therefore advise against rushing a building with concrete floor deckings in three months (too short a time!). Conversely, there is a level of construction you can get to, that time is of essence to continue or else damage could set in to things you have previously achieved. This applies to buildings under construction that have been left off, almost abandoned in that uncompleted state for long period (maybe due to lack of finance). In these respects listen to you builders advise.

BUILDING STAGES AT A GLANCE

1. **Foundation** – setting out / excavation / concrete blinding / block work / German flooring / damp proof coursing / footing for columns.

2. **Walls** – external load bearing walls / internal partitions.

3. **Lintels** – window openings / door openings.

4. **Levels** – roof beams / upper floor decking.

5. **Roofing (if bungalow)** – carpentry works for timber / roofing covering – slates, asbestos sheets, iron sheet, longspan aluminum.

6. **Upper floor decking (detached houses / multi storey)** – timber form work / props / reinforcements – 10mm, 12mm, 14mm, 16mm steel bars / concrete overlay.

7. **Ceiling** – P.O.P / asbestos / cellotex boards / plastics / other synthetic materials.

8. **Plastering** – internal and external. The rooms, sitting room, all require smooth plastering. Te bathrooms and kitchen may be plastered rough if they will be finished with ceramic tiles.

9. **Flooring** – quite a variety of floor finishes – timber / wood, terrazzo / ceramic tiles / porcelain / marble / granite / rubber tiles.

10. **Windows** – louvers, aluminum profiles - anodized, powder coated, plastic or vinyl, Critall-Hope or metal frames, glazed timber framed.

11. **Doors** – timber / wood / aluminum, steel (bullet proof) imported pre-pressed steel.

12. **Plumbing works** – pipe network – plumbing fittings, faucets, bath tubs, w.c toilets, wash hand basin, bidet, shower units, Jacuzzi, kitchen sink.

13. **Electrical works** – conduit wiring, electrical fittings – sockets, light points, switches, airconditioner points, tv sockets, intercom sockets, gas cooker socket (kitchen)

14. **Painting** – internally and externally – textcote, water – based paint (emulsion), oil based paint (gloss).

15. **Iron Mongery** – burglar proofing, steel door fabrication, external gates.

16. **External works** – boys quarter construction, landscape, garden, mass concrete, interlocking pavements.

Quite a long list and almost intimidating but it all starts with taking the first step. It is like the old Chinese proverb that says the journey of a thousand miles begins with one step.

People have done it for ages. The only thing that changes are the materials used in the building as technology evolves new designs and sophistication. Ask an average landlord aged sixty or seventy years how they achieved building in their time and you will discover that it was even more gradual in their own days.

Prepare To Build!

Take a deep breath – you are about to start building. Even if you are normally a laid back person with many other issues, you now need to become proactive. Building needs your attention and if you really think about it, what you put in is what you get! It is for your future comfort, so give it what it takes.

- **Start recognizing your time** to accommodate the time you need to minimally oversee your property being developed.

- **Tidy up on the issue of resource and financing.** The flow of money must not dry up and deep down you must be convinced that it won't. No one else can determine this for you because you are the one who knows your circumstances. If you depend on your pay for constant money flow, then keep your job well. If you depend on your business profits to keep money flowing, work harder now than before. If you need to structure your building pace to meet your target saving (ajo), please do so fairly accurately. Later on in the book, there are portions that further deal with how you can raise the stakes by growing your money to a good level before applying it to building. We will also examine how we can use cooperatives to advantage.

Even God envisaged this is His word. The Bible asks – What kind of man would want to build a house and would not first count the cost? He will get stuck halfway and become the object of mockery.

This is not contradictory to the earlier motivations you have received. In fact it is enhancing because it is not enough to start and get stuck – you need to see the project through and that is often based on good and thorough foresight.

The summer of this simply means that while you may not conceivably have all the money for your building right from inception, have some, enough to have a good start. Then, you need to be able to at least foresee how the rest could possibly come, in the nearest future – period!

- **Based on the above, you must now decide what house type you want (or can afford!).** The undoing of some people is not being candid enough to stick to their level. They go for house types that their income cannot possibly support and eventually fail to achieve completion. Such people remain in rented apartments and own this huge edifice of a house that has been stuck at roofing stage for years. It is no use to them. Why won't such a person go for a bungalow from the word go? Everyone must consider so many things, including the maintenance factor after you have moved in. your personal house will still make demands on your income after you move in. since it yields no income, it can be a financial burden if not well managed. (There are good descriptions of various house types in the book, *How To Buy Property Safely in Nigeria,* that can help your decision on a house that fits budget.) Remember this – people get stuck when they become too ambitious with building size. You must be in touch with reality.

Make Contact With Some Professionals

The Land Surveyor

Obviously one of the first you will need because you must survey your plot of land. Surveyors are trained to properly (scientifically) demarcate land boundaries. The first benefit is that you know the extent of your boundaries and if some other person has encroached on your land, you will be told. You now have proper beacons (the surveyor's work is not complete if he does not put beacons with numbers). Beacons are the small square shaped concrete points you see at the corners of plots, more easily observed in undeveloped plots. Survey plans are compulsory because you cannot obtain town planning approval without them.

Make sure you approach a registered land surveyor to avoid repeated spending as there are many quacks parading as land surveyors. If you use a quack, you will soon realize that there is no "red copy" in the government record on your survey and you have to do it again.

The Architect

Here is the person who will bring reality to your dream by designing and drawing whatever you ask (as long as you are willing to pay). Avoid draughtsmen who can draw like the architect but are not trained to design like a registered architect. Many draughtsmen will claim to have the architect's skills bit it is not true. It is a case of wrapping cakes of soap with leaves for prolonged periods and the leaves become like soap! For best results, ask round for an architectural firm registered with the NIA – Nigeria Institute of Architects. Furthermore, without the stamp of a registered architect, your plan will not be given the necessary Town Planning approval.

Civil/Structural Engineer

It is not usual for individuals to look around for structural engineers for single residential building projects. The architect would normally sort this out. You require engineering drawings showing the design frame of the building. The network of beams and columns (upright and reinforced pillars) that will carry the building that the architect has designed for you.

Note of warning: Sometimes the architect stretches his creative imagination so much that the cost implications become rather high. You do not need such designs that drastically increase the steel and concrete contents of your building. It will only cost you more money and aggravate your finances. Ask questions about details because the structural man will design around the architect's work and it may involve massive structures.

The Quantity Surveyor

For some odd reasons, a lot of people have not discovered the usefulness of a cost estimator. A quantity surveyor will give you a small document of few pages called the Bill of Quantities. This informs you of how much your entire building should cost and the quantity of materials you may likely use. He works with the architectural drawings. The document is a very useful guide.

First, the builder or his workmen cannot take you on a ride and of course you also know that plus (+) or minus (-) your house should not cost more than X figure. The reason most people shy away from engaging a Quantity Surveyor is because of fees. Look, approach one first and make it plain that you do not want to spend much money in fees because you have not even started building. Every building professional in Nigeria appreciates this and should give you a good document at affordable fees. Mark this – you will save more money by having a document to consult at every stage of the building that you receive quotes from workmen.

For instance at roofing stage you are given a quote by the carpenter for the timber you need before the roof covering. Look here, it is all gibberish to you – 200 (No) of 3 x 4 / 420 (No) of 2 x 2 / 300 (No) of 2 x 6. If you do not have facts you just toss around restlessly and beat cost wildly and then release money in exasperation when you reduce the sum to the level that you feel comfortable with. There is nothing scientific about what you have just done. The timber supplier, or roof man or contractor or whatever he calls himself will still have his way. He may have heavily inflated the quantity such that you cannot cut it too low.

Did you say you will count? You may soon get tired of counting even if you resume to the site daily before going to work. Play it smart – this method works – trim down the quote with the help of a Bill of Quantities and your work gets done. You see, there is a psychology of the workmen you have on site. Majority of them are NOT outright thieves in the sense that they bolt away with your money – NO. They are smart enough to know that they still need you and more contracts through you. What they have devised is native intelligence to get more out of you and by implication, slow down your project. It is like the story of rats that infest people's houses, nibbles at their fingers while they are asleep and blow cool air so they won't feel the bite!

They benefit hugely from the cost of materials and still charge you full labour. This is the sort of thing you may encounter at every stage of work. This is the reason why many people abandon ship and are discouraged from building. This is also the reason why the outright solution is being offered to you to prevent your giving up. From the moment you firm up, things will surely work better. Now, do not get too rigid by tightening up so much that not even one crumb will fall to the ground from your table – NO. this is not possible in self-build efforts anywhere in the world. You can only minimize such losses to a limit of say 5 – 10%.

Choosing Your Builder

The choice of a builder is very crucial to the experience you will have in construction. It may turn out pleasant or very unpleasant and it all depends on what choices you make at this crucial point. Some people have been misled to pick the wrong builder before and ended up with a collapsed building under construction. Given the right weight, these things are avoidable from the onset. At some other time, the structure is alright but the cost is prohibitive because the builder is taking more for himself and putting less in the building.

Note: Building is a skill and the builder ought to translate the architect's drawing into physical reality. Good construction whether in progress or after completion showcase the builders skill. Poor construction is also easy to spot because the signs are mostly obvious on the building fabric (except for structural faults).

It is in your interest to look for a skilled builder and it takes searching and knowing what to look out for.

- A builder should have appropriate building related qualifications.
- A builder should have undergone training or pupilage in a building firm/outfit that he effortlessly

discloses. The way to know is if he hesitates before telling you where he is coming from. It may be alright to double check. This is a life-long investment you are about to entrust to somebody.

- A builder should come to you based on the recommendation of a satisfied client(s) whose work has recently been finished and you can view it. In fact, a useful starting point is to ask among your peers, friends and relatives for a builder. As you view his work you can basically appreciate the level of his skill. If in doubt get a second opinion before you engage the builder.

- It may help to observe if several worthy clients are also giving work to the same builder. How many projects does he have on hand? Alternatively, how many projects has he recently completed? (builders sometimes misguide in order to win a new job and point out projects they did not execute, so double check.)

- Some builders are good but tend to be expensive. This may be obvious from the class of clientele he serves. There are builders who only build for bankers and oil company workers. An average civil servant may not bother to engage such a person.

- Sometimes a bricklayer is introduced as a builder by a well meaning friend based on work done before. May be after viewing the work done you are uncomfortable about it but cannot place exactly what is wrong, you do not have to engage this builder. Do not yield to pressure in cases where you cannot see past work done or assess his track record.

- Most cases of poor building work result from not investigating the builder before engaging him. Investigating the builder is not necessarily a fool proof approach but it helps to limit outright blunders.

- Compatibility is also important to your choice of a builder. Since you will be working closely together your temperaments must be agreeable. Decline a builder who has an attitude even if people claim he is very good. He may stand you up midway in the project. Avoid someone who has airs about him. Usually such builders lack work ethics.

- This task of selecting a builder is not easy. Word of mouth helps locate the right builder, then watch him for honesty, promptness, good attitude. It is after these that you can possibly engage such a person to start. Why give mobilization or money for part supply of building materials to a man who you cannot trace if he disappears? Always have links and references.

- Lastly, do not hesitate to fire a builder if you discover you made a mistake, especially on the issue of dishonesty or poor skills. Your reason must be strong because the devil you know is better than the devil you do not know. Sounds like they are both devil anyway!

  For balance try making an arrangement to have your architect and structural engineer represented on site for crucial periodical inspections when work has commenced. They will often straighten the builder up. Believe it

PLANNING APPROVALS

Obtaining approval from the town planning section of the authorities in charge of wherever your land is situated is a basic prerequisite to starting your building. There are rules that guide this task and a list of typical requirements for submission. They usually include the following.

1. A specified number of sets of architectural drawings.
2. Copies of survey plan.
3. Payment of assessment/fees.

The drawings must observe setbacks, plot ratio and contain structural drawings. They must also bear the stamp and seal of the Architect and Engineer. Never mind if the approval takes sometimes to process before the authorities finally consent to your building. It is better to have it in place before construction starts. **An organized person who recognizes the possibility of planning approval delays should start the process months before, so it is co-terminus with building start.**

Institutions that carry out inspections / approvals are:

- Local Government offices – Town Planning Section
- State Government offices – Town Planning Department
- State Housing Corporation – Town Planning Department
- State/Local Government Property Investment Company – Town Planning Department

- New Town Development Authorities – Town Planning Department

- Development Control Offices (e.g. Abuja, FCT) – Town Planning Department.

- Federal Housing Authority (FHA) – Town Planning Department.

- Federal Capital Development Authority (FCDA) – Town Planning Department.

- Federal Ministry of Works (FMW) – Town Planning Department.

- Some Private Developers – Town Planning Department.

The approving authority you approach will depend on where your land is located and who controls the area. display the approval number visibly on your construction site by writing boldly to avoid constant harassment by inspection officers from Town Planning authorities in the area.

Can't Cope – I Prefer To Pay Someone Else To Handle Things

The only other way to build apart from incremental building is to contract is out of rapid results. This is most suitable for anyone who does not have the patience and temperament for building through self supervision. Certainly it goes without saying that such people must have good funds to compensate for their impatience or else they have got to learn the patience to go through the rigors of incremental building.

In a way, the idea being peddled really is that you can outsource all these details of your building work. Whether they are preparatory works before actual construction, like town planning approval, obtaining estimates or buying construction materials, someone else can do them on your behalf. The same applies to actual building. A contract builder can construct your house from start to finish on an agreed figure and give a time/date for completion as long as money is released at each stage of building that funds are required. There are various forms of contract builders that exist for each person to work with. It depends on your preference.

Just few years back in Lagos, the concept of *design and build* was rather popular and a lot of young successful men climbing up the corporate ladder engaged these people to design a house for them. The same designer goes ahead to build (a sort of turnkey arrangement). Today maybe the only

It is advisable to use a builder's expertise to erect your structure. So, the concept of building incrementally should not be interpreted to mean that it is Do-It-Yourself (DIY). Otherwise you end up with a contraption that won't pass a beauty test. However, you are paying fees or labour charges for the builder to apply his core skills directly to raise your building from foundation to finish.

thing that has changed is that people have titled towards getting more involved with their house design. Eventually, they contract the construction aspect out (materials and labour) and only visit regularly to see that the house is coming up the way they went.

This method no doubt will turn out more costly than the gradual, incremental building process. In effect, you are hiring someone else, presumably competent, to do all the tasks of organizing and supervision that you would have done yourself. But why not, if you lack the time or interest and you have enough funds to pay!

In the process of deciding which way to go something must be made clear. It is advisable to use a builder's expertise to erect your structure. So, the concept of building incrementally should not be interpreted to mean that it is Do-It-Yourself (DIY). Otherwise you end up with a contraption that won't pass a beauty test. However, you are paying fees or labour charges for the builder to apply his core skills directly to raise your building from foundation to finish. And this, you can agree upon in stages as it suits you and your pocket. All other things like buying materials, running around for approvals, chasing up other workers (plumber/electrician, etc.) are done by you.

In the alternative being discussed now, not only do you engage the builder's core competence in building, he is hired to do all the runnings you would have done. This leaves him carrying all the responsibility of seeing the building through and he gets paid for it. People who use this method would usually have attained a certain comfort level. It would cost you an average 20% to 30% above actual building cost to send a building cost to send a builder on errand if it is well priced. Unfortunately due to lack of proper documentation and the informal method of handling such contracts, cost levels could be more than you bargained for (sometimes more than 50% above, which means you need only half the money spent to achieve your building).

Both methods have their merits and demerits. Individual choices are also based on each person's circumstances and money considerations. If you can afford it why not have someone else do your dirty hard work!

Your Income Sources

This is part of the reality of becoming an adult and coming of age. Coming this far in the book is a clear indication that you take this subject seriously. In fact you have been sucked in and find that you have a clearer picture of what it takes to achieve home ownership. It is now time to give an account of what you have done so far with income analysis. What is your financial position? What have you saved so far? Can you apply it all to build? Can you save more money as you earn since you are soon going to exhaust your current savings as you build?

It is now time to put to use the exercise under the Action Plan Module 1. Which is your determined source (or sources) of income?

- Employed
- Self-employed/formal or informal sector

- Business owner/entrepreneur

- Investor

Hopefully you have a savings pattern that works for you now. By achieving this feat, you now have a pool of funds that can be applied to building no matter how small or big. Somehow it is expected that from your savings, you have also been able to buy a plot of land as you prepared to build. If you have a income and you have been unable to achieve this level so far, perhaps you lack commitment. If you have some savings but are still not willing to commit it to build then you still may not understand that building successfully is about having a real estate investment habit. Little drops of water makes an ocean.

The way each group will eventually build may differ because of their income source which affects their saving pattern. This has serious effects on the quality of house you can afford, the length of time it will take to complete the

It is interesting to observe that with much lower sums of consistent savings, many have achieved home ownership; sometimes faster than higher income earners. You may call it "building by design" or "the science of house building" but the way you earn money surely reveals how you can personally raise

house and the method you will need to employ to build (incremental method or contract or a hybrid of the two).

Someone who can save N200,000 monthly for building can plan to spend N2.4 million every year on his house – this is fairly predictable and the only thing he has to worry about is the rising price of building materials due to inflation. Contrast this with an example of a self employed service provider in the informal sector whose earning depends on how hard the works and if he is fortunate to get clients. He saved N380,000 in the first quarter of the year, didn't get serious jobs commitments until the last quarter when he saved another N500,000.

Unlike our first example, this person has only succeeded in saving N880,000 partly because of the unpredictability and irregularity of his income. Both persons can build – what differs is the way each one will need to go about it, to achieve maximum results. Also the timing of completion may differ since one has more consistent savings than the other.

This has led to the following classification which is a suggested approach based on each person's vocational differences. The figures used so far are for illustration only. It is interesting to observe that with much lower sums of consistent savings, many have achieved home ownership; sometimes faster than higher income earners. You may call it **"building by design"** or **"the science of house building"** but the way you earn money surely reveals how you can personally raise the much needed finance for building.

WAY 1: BUILDING – BY THE SALARY EARNER

This is one group of income earners that should find it easy to build because of the consistency of their earnings. After all, thirty days make one pay!

There are:

- Low income earners
- High income earners

Low income earners usually exhibit the behavior of a Type 2 Profile in Module 1 and averagely tend to achieve home ownership faster than high income earners. Why? It is just about focus. It is the focus that propels them to use up all their micro savings to build!

Imagine a messenger in a university who has built his own house, while the head of department, a professor of good standing still lives in the staff quarters and plays tennis over drinks in the evening without giving serious thought to home ownership. The professor is caught up in his comfort zone! Most of such individuals such as the professor who fit this illustration wait until they are close to retirement before being jolted into the reality of where they will spend their retirement. Most times they start building a house late in life and end up designing a huge edifice they no longer require (since their children have all grown up and left home). They eventually create further problems by their actions.

For the salary earner to build, he is better off using incremental building method.

1. With this, he gets into a systematic saving pattern and knows what is available quarterly, bi-monthly or annually for him to use in building.

2. He can proceed to buy a plot of land with his savings

> *After a while when building has commenced for the salary earner, this thing becomes addictive. He does not need to be sermonized anymore as he builds incrementally. His every focus is unleashed on the site and he knows the difference that adding a mere ten thousand naira will make to his construction efforts.*

and prepare to commence construction going through

all the pre-construction details of building design, survey and town planning approvals.

3. Stage by stage, the salary earner funds periodically from his savings directly on his building project and stops every time money is exhausted.

4. Midway in-between, the salary earner learns to maintain his building site by constant weeding to avoid overgrowth and this occupies him as he faithfully save to start again after few months.

5. Using the method of incremental building is so resourceful. The salary earner appreciates that once a stage is achieved it is the next that follows and the house always takes better form.

6. After a while when building has commenced for the salary earner, this thing becomes addictive. He does not need to be sermonized anymore as he builds incrementally. His every focus is unleashed on the site and he knows the difference that adding a mere ten thousand naira will make to his construction efforts. The truth is, until you get there and experience it yourself, you hardly know what the feeling is like.

HIGH FLYERS – COMPANY EXECUTIVES/EMMIGRATED NIGERIANS

Among the salary earners, are top company employees and senior management or even board members. Many of these workers earn stupendous seven and eight figure salaries yearly. Close on their heels are Nigerians working professionally abroad or others who are mainly economic migrants busy wiring part of their savings home.

Clearly, money or financial muscle to build is not really the challenge being posed to this group. It is the time to devote to supervising yourself build effort since you work schedule leaves no time for any other thing but work and business meetings. (Even your children do not see you during the week because they are asleep by the time you come home every week day! They say "Daddy only comes home weekends".)

Building gradually or incrementally is out of the question. You are better off in this category if you contract out your building. The greatest challenge is getting a trusted building firm or individual who will deliver without swindling you. Whatever you do, get a recommended builder – avoid casual selection of a builder. Document every stage and keep a file (follow all the leads on Choosing Your Builder).

Nigerians living abroad also have this challenge. Unfortunately, many have trusted family members to build for them in the past only to discover later that the building for which they have fully paid has not left foundation level. This is very tragic and there is no foolproof solution to suggest. Even if you have a contractor you still want to have someone watch what is being built on your behalf. What most people get is two of them colluding to siphon your hard earned resources.

A common bend that some people abroad use nowadays is to devote their summer holidays to come to Nigeria, get involved with their building contractor and move the building construction forward as far as possible. Wherever they stop, the work continues the next year because they return ti Nigeria once they get another summer break. It works as a good control measure because as they release the money they are around to watch it turn into brick and mortar! End of storey.

WAY 2: BUILDING – BY THE SELF-EMPLOYED
PROFESSIONAL

This is a very wide group of people. Most professionals whether in this country or anywhere else offer professional services and earn a fee. It can therefore be very rewarding to qualify as a professional and not a few had to train hard in college and professional institutes to qualify. Some years back, it was reported that single girls in Hong Kong expressed first preference for professionals as life partners before any other group because they were the most promising and wealthy.

Well, back to reality. Most professional in Nigeria are having a tough time. The system does not necessarily respect or support professionalism and a lot of professional's therefore mostly earn inconsistently. For such professionals, the issue of building their own house is not easy.

- The professionals who earn the most are those with contacts in the right places. Such people would usually have regular lump sums in fees, part of which can be devoted to build. Such people that enjoy regular patronage can engage a building contractor and pay them for their services. Such group of professionals do not need to build incrementally but they are relatively few in number.

- Some professionals operate in the building industry. They have the privilege of applying their skills and knowledge directly into their own building effort. Not only this, they also attract the input of other colleagues to successfully build. Such operatives of the building industry include architects, quantity surveyors, civil engineers, builders, estate surveyors and valuers and land surveyors, etc. these usually build using the incremental method and because of their knowledge and skills, save cost.

- The majority of professionals in our system however do not fit into the two above. They do not earn regular lump sum fees and are not building industry operatives. Such professionals earn pay cheques far in-between, and because they have to incur overhead/operating costs they may not have much left to save. For these, building may take a little longer and most certainly be done incrementally. Such professionals can greatly benefit from the money growing methods shared later in the book. Interestingly, it is this latter group of professionals who build quicker that others because they drive themselves harder, recognizing their relatives disadvantages.

WAY 3: BUILDING – BY THE ENTREPRENEUR – BUSINESS OWNER

This heading involves a great number of people. They are the informal sector and extend from the small business owner to big business concerns. They span the small traders who operate at the lower end of the retail trade to significant indigenous trading companies, importers and exporters, haulage companies, small commuter bus operators and so on.

The way Nigeria is structured, this group actually powers the largely unregulated portions of the economy and too many people fits here. It is therefore critical that people who are traders, entrepreneurs or business owners in this system are shown how they can build their own house because it can translate to significant increases in the nation's housing stock.

The desire and preference to trade by many Nigerians is intrinsic and almost always passed down from one generation to another. This informal school of economics, especially at the low end of the retail chain has taught even the small trader that you must plough back your profit to grow. Everyone with a little capital wants to sell something to tap from a huge 120 million people market and it works. But small capital yields little profit and not surprisingly, so many businesses remain at this level, barely surviving. It then becomes unthinkable for many to plan to build a personal house from this small business level.

It is possible for a good portion of traders and small business owners at this level to build if only they can evolve a regular small saving pattern. Some market women after the day's trade can save a thousand naira daily. In fact some already do this in the cooperative and thrift society they belong to. Why can't they evolve such a saving pattern specifically for building?

Most people in this category are usually mindful of taking money out of their trading profits. They equally guard against eating into their small business capital. But you have to face the fact – nothing goes for nothing. You increase your personal security when you can have a property of your own. Come to think of it, your bank may even become willing to inject funds into your business when you can point a real estate of your own collateral. So it's worth the extra push for you to save and divert some money towards this.

The careful balance is achieving this building effort over time, without crippling your trade which is where the money is coming from anyway. Usually bank credit is not available to most people at this level and once capital is depleted, their earning power is gone. The business stops and the building stop as well –

> *That is why, for the entrepreneur and business owner – big or small – the building process has to be a planned, deliberate action that takes out just a little profit at a time for building.*

uncompleted. This would be an undesirable result.

In fact, in some fewer instances some businessmen who have access to bank credit have processed loans. The loans were primarily approved to be injected into their business at commercial rates and they wrongly apply it to building a personal house. Of course, the loan has to be rapid but the business cannot pay it back since it was not invested there in the first instance. That is why, for the entrepreneur and business owner – big or small – the building process has to be a planned, deliberate action that takes out just a little profit at a time for building.

For sure the incremental method of building is most applicable here. At every stage small amounts taken from profit are applied to building from foundation to roofing until the house is successfully completed.

WAY 4: BUILDING – BY THE INVESTOR

For the investor his approach to building is a whole new paradigm, entirely guided by a different set of considerations. Hard core investors think about profit, profit and profit (remember the core investor made popular by the ongoing privatization exercise!). The investor's primary concern therefore is always watching to see how he can turn brick and mortar into fantastic returns that can compare with the kind of profits he has made hitherto from other trades as well.

There are two broad outlines of ways the investor usually achieves this. The first is the **investor builder** and the other is the **merchant builder.** Any attempt by an investor to coin a new name or use a different appellation and re-invent the wheel really ends up under these two headings upon closer scrutiny. It is all about making choices after due considerations, depending on overall policy and objectives, and of course, the niche market.

The investor builder is one who builds to let/lease and is happy to take rents annually from the tenants until the project pays back. This is usually concentrated in areas or urbanities where returns on rent are very good and justify the heavy cost incurred in new development. Areas like Lagos Island – Ikoyi, Victoria Island are viable for the investor builder who can charge as high as 60,000 US Dollars per annum for a single flat in a luxury block that may contain twenty flats! This trend is also becoming visible in a city like Port Harcourt where oil companies can lease the entire block of high-rise flats in the GRA (Government Reservation Area) thereby justifying the investor efforts.

The merchant builder essentially builds to sell. He has evolved a system that churns out houses into the housing market for sale. Gradually he has become more familiar with his market – people who fall into the income bracket that can afford to buy his houses. People who are in the category of merchant builders are often called developers. Now the term developer is equally appropriated because the developer equally develops for profit. Anyone who builds a development and hands over to another is not a developer but a builder. But the word merchant builder directly indicates a trader of some sort. In this case houses are the product or merchandise being traded.

It is easy to relate to this concept nowadays if you read the newspapers. You find a new estate with various house types advertised boldly for sale. Pick up *The Guardian on Monday,* or the *Punch* – weekends and Mondays or *This Day* newspapers and deliberately count the number of development companies advertising new houses for sale. They are all merchant builders or, in common parlance, developers. This should not be confused with Estate Surveyors and Valuers who advertise properties for sale as a normal trend offering residential, commercial, institutional properties for sale from the property market – such properties that are not necessarily new construction and are mostly owned by individual clients selling for various reasons. They are not deliberate projects built for profit.

The true position is that the investor has a large pool of funds in the bank and earns basic interest only because he operates in his core trade and keeps his funds within the money market. There are money-bags who have made a fortune in this country doing other trades like contracts, supply business and so on. Many at this level are successful business owners but their profit is under-utilised. Some of them have realized it and are yearning to bring it into the property market. With a little guidance from the right consultant they become investor builders and developers.

The investor is not building to satisfy his own needs. He probably already has done so long ago. What he is really doing is to spread his tentacles like an octopus into other areas. And what better area than housing development – hard wearing, long lasting and profitable!

DO SOMETHING!

A final thought as we leave this module. Do away with every excuse you have had so far to stay action. Map out a convincing route to home ownership by what you have been helped to see systematically in this book. Then go for it – do something! Even the greatest business plans fail, not because the idea is not good or the environment is difficult but because of the lack of one ingredient – ACTION!

ACTION PLAN

1. Go ahead to find a friendly architect and then a builder. Start with word of mouth references among friends and associate until you locate the person who you think understands where you are coming from.
   - It is okay for you to discuss fees and charges early to fully appreciate the sort of figures you are looking at. In a way, you also can feel the pulse of the architect and builder early. This helps you to know if you can work with them
2. Design your building properly. The architect may provide you with up to 2-3 design options. Make your

choice not based on fantasy but reality. It can have a serious effect on lowering cost.

3. Do a building material survey. Two things you begin to achieve here. The first is that you begin to know the building materials markets in your locality. You may discover some places you never knew existed before – you now know where to find which materials, electrical, plumbing, sanitary fittings (toilets, baths, etc).

   The second is that you are exposed to a wide variety of materials at different costs. Some are long lasting while other will damage easily. Some are just befitting and equally expensive! While others are plain but good quality and do the job. It is a whole big world of choices and this will help you really think realistically about who you are and what you can achieve with your resource in the immediate sense. As a guide, make a list of common materials you want to check out and boy, are they many!

4. Lastly, search out good artisans now especially electricians, carpenters, plumbers and tillers. You need to get these heading of work right in your house to save yourself of the daily hassles of repairs that are

needed if they are not well done. The safest route is to poke nose, pry into the home of friends and associates so you can use the people that did their house for them as long as they are confirm it is good work done.

MODULE FOUR

AN ARRAY OF POSSIBILITIES

Everyone that has built successfully in this will admit that they had to tap into personal resourcefulness. It is line an adaptation process. The human body can adjust itself to survive in different environments, whether extreme temperatures of heat and cold or serious physical pressure resulting in pain. There are always threats to the body internally and externally and the human body system fights to stay alive with the aid of antibodies, body resistance and immunity.

The task of building may not appear that extreme for some to achieve but considering the lack of credit or financial support from lenders most people have to improvise and make do with limited funds. It is from these hands on experience of others that the following have been inferred. It can work for you if you recognize any method below that excites you.

There is a chain retail store in the United Kingdom called The Pound Stretcher. It is a very fascinating name because it passes its marketing strategy and promise to the customer already by this name. It I s simply telling you to come inside and stretch every single pound sterling that you will spend in order to buy more than it can ordinarily buy elsewhere.

> *The immediate challenge however is how to stretch the naira (just like the pound stretcher) so that less money can accomplish more for you in building. One is just not sure that the naira is as elastic or can be stretched at all.*

In other words you come out of their stores with s bigger basket of goods than your pounds would have gotten somewhere else.

In a sense, this is how each of us applying our seemingly meager resources to building must begin to think.

Building a house at whatever level you are, is one of the largest single spending or purchase an individual will make in a lifetime as earlier pointed out. It would have been okay to borrow part of this large sum and pay it back gradually over time but borrowing has not been made easy yet and most people have to invent a way forward for their savings. In a way it is good because once you have built successfully your house is entirely dept free! The immediate challenge however is how to stretch the naira (just like the pound stretcher) so that less money can accomplish more for you in building. One is not just sure that the naira is as elastic or can be stretch at all. There is a combination of efforts in

It would have been okay to borrow part of this large sum and pay it back gradually over time but borrowing has not been made easy yet and most people have to invent a way forward for their savings. In a way it is good because once you have built successfully your house is entirely dept free!

watching cost, inflation and the flow of funding for building. This has helped others in the past and hopefully should help you, as you build you own dwelling.

Cost Cutting Vs Cost Efficiency.

If building cost can be reduced, many more people will build. Fewer people will get stuck and others will finish their abandoned projects. The element of cost seems to determine everything. In the real active sense, most individuals who engage in building their own house hack at cost and try to cut down on whatever the work men are demanding. It can be very frustrating because rather than succeed at cutting costs, most of the time prices of building materials and labour are going up. Yet you struggle to keep up and see the house through to completion.

Cost cutting and cost efficiency are a combination of

Cost cutting and cost efficiency are a combination of two approaches that can significantly lower what it will cost to build your own house.

two approaches that can significantly lower what it will cost to build your own house. Of course, if you can achieve this, it is possible to complete your house in a much shorter time. Also you only spend a fraction of what others are spending.

By the above, what this means, is that two similar houses that look almost exact in finishes may differ significantly in cost. If Mr Osagie built his four bedroom bungalow for N4.8 million in year 2005, Mr Malik may spend N6 million on a similar bungalow also built in the same year. There is a whopping 25 % differential in cost, although they used the same method to build, which is serious. Now many things can account for this, which is why the implications are being examined so as to help everyone manage building costs better.

No doubt a difference in construction time as much as one year in-between can account for a sharp rise in total cost. This is usually caused by inflation in our country which still has one of the highest inflation rates in the world. Building materials cost goes up with every fuel price hike or change in import policy. Labour costs also rise sharply- it starts with the artisans who will demand increased daily wages to allow for whatever public transporters are now charging.

This is what gives rise to a local myth#1- No one can really ever calculate the cost of his house from start to finish.

This myth has gained grounds because it is most people's experience that once you start (and most build incrementally from savings as you know), costs keep changing with time, month after month, year after year. Depending on the time in-between the cost variation may be little or much. The unpredictability of these marginal increase is what fuels this belief which is somehow true.

This is however not the reason for the 25% cost difference in the example involving Messrs Osagie and Malik which is why the underlying study of the cause and effect of escalated building costs will help to work things better.

Cost Efficiency

For a building to be cost efficient, all cost savings must be factored in from planning stage, long before actual construction. Consciously or unconsciously, the choices you make add up to cost. For the skillful in building, this is easily turned to advantage and a few of the positive moves that ensure a cost efficient building are examined below.

- **The type of building matters** - a bungalow for instance will cost less than a detached house on two floors. While a bungalow involves a basic foundation (strip foundation) if it is on good soil, it goes ahead with walls coming up quickly up to lintel and roofing. In no time the house is being finished. A house on two floors however, will involve structural preparation right from foundation – reinforced steel as base mats for several columns; a network of columns and beams to carry the concrete decking- the cost of the decking itself and so on. Want a building that is efficient on cost?. Choose a bungalow design.

- **Shapes cost money.** When the architect has designed, there are many beautiful shapes and strokes in design that simple blockwork cannot accomplish. It has to be cast in concrete and probably reinforced. Compared to straight blockwork such as the walls of the building (superstructure) these are much more expensive. Do not forget that even the carpenter will have to build the formwork first before concrete is cast. Even if you do not really catch the details, question your structure along these lines. The architect and structural engineer should catch your drift and help with realistic adjustment.

- **To achieve efficiency, things as basic as the slope of the land you will purchase need to be factored in.** Even the soil texture. If the slope is very sharp, it will involve retaining walls. This is certainly several times more costly than a simple foundation on flat ground and it impacts on overall cost. Areas with sandfilling or soil of very soft texture require what is called a raft foundation. This involves a steel mesh (just like the decking) with a lot of concrete work, all of which is very expensive.

- **Cantilevers** can be very expensive because they significantly increase the steel content of the building and consequently the cost of building goes up. The greater the cantilever width or span, the greater the steel content and cost associated with it.

- **Big buildings have cost implications.** From experience most novices cannot appreciate the size of a building from the drawings. The building is up before they realize it is too big. Do not allow this to happen to you. Instead, familiarize yourself with lengths and measurements by comparing lengths in the drawings with actual buildings like the one you presently live in.

  - Bigger room sizes have cost implications. Check each detail.

  - If the building is on two floors, the span of the upper floor decking increases with larger rooms. Now smaller spans can do with 12mm rods but wider spans will require 16mm rods. And if there are cantilevers, the number of 6mm rods needed goes up! To achieve cost efficiency, you need first of all to realize this difference, weigh its implication on your family's accommodation needs and adjust. This little adjustment can achieve significant cost reduction.

- The word efficiency in the sense in which it is used to relate to building costs here means spending money on your building and deriving maximum benefit in terms of output. The way to achieve this is to critically observe every part of the building before construction starts. The cost input into each part may be reduced by simple changes in design or usage of building materials (just as illustrated above with the example of iron rods). All of these little things will add up to substantial savings at the end of your construction effort.

- To drive home the point on cost efficiency even better, some people use a careful combination of 9-inch and 6-inch blocks in building to save money. Now, 9- inch blocks come recommended in building all external walls because they carry the weight of the upper floor decking or the roof-they are called load bearing walls.

Internal walls are used to demarcate the rooms, toilets and kitchen can be 6-inch walls since they usually bear no load but a lot of us use 9- inch blocks throughout. It however gives the fell of a stronger building. However, efficient cost savers insist on using 9- inch blocks in the right places and will use 6-inch blocks in the right places as well, saving the little margin of cost between the two. It may seem negligible but it is part of achieving cost efficiency.

The moment you are spending lavishly on your building you must have it somewhere at the back of your mind that you are not achieving cost efficiency. First you are probably spending to buy the best of every material and this does not ensure that you get the best output for every cost input necessarily. Also the most lavish finishing is not necessarily the best as

The way to achieve this is to critically observe every part of the building before construction starts. The cost input into each part may be reduced by simple changes in design or usage of building materials (just as illustrated above with the example of iron rods).

most people may think. A good combination of decent choices will do.

Cost Cutting

Just as the heading suggests, this is the effort of cutting down prices and charges as actual construction is going on. There is some progression already from the stage of design and planning in which you watched out keenly for a cost efficient building. Now the focus is on trying to make sure that as you actually build, you spend less money to achieve more. By the end of the exercise, you can successfully save between 20% and 50% of total building costs.

Even though it is a painstaking effort, it pays off because money you would have spent at a particular stage is conserved to take construction work a little further. For instance, if you save money by cutting costs on roof covering whether it is corrugated asbestos sheets or long span aluminum. The savings are quantifiable when you subtract what the materials averagely cost in the building materials market from what you actually paid. If you avoided the popular timber market in town and bought cheaper from a sawmill out of town, your savings will be clear.

Some people approach cost cutting wrongly and mess up there entire building effort. Worse still, it is this same cost cutting that leads to several building collapse in various parts of the country. This is the tragedy of ignorantly cutting costs.

WHAT COST CUTTING IS NOT.

- Using substandard and inferior building materials merely because they work out cheaper is NOT cost cutting.

- Employing professionals and builders based on how much they agree to accept is NOT cost cutting. They must be skilled and qualified.

- Cost cutting is NOT cutting down on the quantity of materials needed at any stage. This may result in cracks and structural failure, when materials are spread too thinly.

- Reducing the strength of concrete is NOT cost cutting. Concrete is a mixture of sand, gravel cement hydrolised by adding water. It is a major material used in building. It is usually for a specified ratio either 1:2:4 or1:3:6 or 1:4:8 depending on where the concrete is to be used. The professionals know best and detail where to use it and you, the owner or client should not change it indiscriminately.

Successful cost is based on knowing the building process and updating current market prices. You need to be very practical to significantly cut costs and still end up with a good house. Feel free to follow some of the following strategy.

First of all, it is vital to locate the source of supply of all the major building materials. By this, you accomplish two things- you can immediately know how much things are sold. This makes it impossible for workmen to inflate costs to deceive you. Secondly, you will locate various sources for each building materials type and discover the best sources for value. You may find some part of town is best for electrical fittings, while ceramic tiles are cheaper on another street. Subtly, all these influence you as you slash costs brought for your approval. Make sure you bargain hard to know the lowest prices acceptable in the market.

- Locate several sandcrete block makers

- Know where tippers for sand, gravel, laterite and granite locate.

- Find out where the cement depot is, in town – depots usually offer the best prices.

- Where are the sawmills located in your area? You may soon discover that prices can differ for the same wood type.

Inevitably, a good knowledge of the building materials market will lead to cost savings for you because you easily cope with accurate costing and will tend not to pay for things at inflated costs.

Always trim down on quotes based on knowledge. This is close to the above because it depends on you having a fair idea of prices. If you do not know what a particular building material currently costs you can quickly do a survey by visiting the market best known for the stage of work you are building. If you cannot go, send somebody else. This is especially important if you are paying your builder in stages- labour and materials. It will certainly lead you to substantial cost savings.

o **Bargain on quantity.** In the retail world, the trader is attracted to lowering price if the quantity bought is high. You can use this to advantage sometimes as building progresses. Items like blocks, cement, timber, ceramics, plumbing materials, can be cheaper when bought in bulk. Use this to advantage where you can.

   Understand also that if you save up and execute your house building project by stages, you can actually buy bulk materials for that stage. For example, you can purchase and store all the cement required to plaster your walls inside out and achieve some discount while pushing your work forward by a good leap. This is one clear stage dealt with before you pick on another.

o **On-site savings.** Little things count while building on site. It is common for people to rent headpans, diggers, shovels, hammers for what looks like little amounts daily. The interesting thing is that cumulatively, you will rent these items for many weeks. If you calculate and add up what you pay for rent in two weeks, it could pay for new ones. Why not buy your own stuff and use them for the duration of your construction? You can either sell them as secondhand after completion or give them away you save a lot by buying your own work tools.

Also there are some items you can mange well by repeat usage while building. Things like fibre used for formwork to cast german flooring can be kept for the lintels formwork. The timber used for the decking can be useful for roof beams and lintels. The bamboo used as props may become useful as scaffolds for plastering the walls and so on. Learn not to waste anything on site. Excavations from foundation and septic tank/soakaway and maybe deep water well can be used for backfilling the foundation to damp proof course (DPC) instead of buying laterite.

o **Use direct labour** only if you know what each worker should accomplish daily. The eddicient use of labour is achieved only if the worker put in what is traditionally accepted as his daily quota. On the average however, most artisans do less per day when they spot the opportunity, so that the same task will take more time to finish, therefore earning more money. A bricklayer plastering walls should plaster two sides of walls in a room of average size in our part of the world. You need to know such things and variations of it so you can get the best out of daily paid workers.

Alternatively, bargain with your builder on paying per stage to avoid workers cheating you if they are paid daily. This way, you can drive a hard bargain at each stage of construction work (you will see how your builder will in turn drive his own workers daily). Take your time to bargain the labour for each stage with your builder, understanding that it also includes something for his efforts. Don't be stampeded into approving just anything handed to you as labour cost.

- **Lastly supervise personally!**

Be involved. Keeps an eagle sharp eye on work being done. Depending on the nature of your job, work out a way of temporarily fitting your building supervision into your routine. The more absent you are, the easier it is for you to lose a hold on cost. Your presence reduces pilferages, wastage and use of poor substandard, materials in the place of the substandard, materials in the place of the standard which you paid for. Truly you cannot be there all the time, but know that the few times you are present makes quite some difference.

- If it is proving too difficult to be there personally, **get someone trusted to be your eyes** – a younger brother, trusted friend or worker while you still work on your personal calculations personally.

- **Labour siphons money.** Standardise labour by determining what they should do daily.

- **Simplify your processes to be as direct as possible.** A complex will allow internal your processes to be as direct as possible. A complex will allow internal your processes to be as direct as possible. A complex will allow internal your processes to be as direct as possible. A complex will allow internal fraud. For instance keeping a large store containing too many materials at the same time on site is risky. Most likely you will require a store keeper or site clerk and a process for taking materials out. This should be minimize to storing only what you can use at ongoing stage. If you have to store other materials to beat cost, fine a place at your present residence to keep them until required.

- **Remember, cost cutting takes you far on small sums.**

UNCONVENTIONAL COST REDUCTION

In a bid to save costs, other building other building systems have been developed all over the world.   These have recorded varying levels of success in different countries. Some people use pre-cast concrete walling, or prefabricated metal, timber, or resins to build. All these record various degrees of acceptance in these countries depending on their

> *Some simply assembly the bricks in an interlocking form (saving cost of mortar) and even where structures are necessary they employ few iron rods. The degree of cost cutting achievable will vary but it said to be substantial. The only problem is that not enough people have tried it and told others.*

social make-up and culture.

Attempts to introduce alternative cost saving building methods in Nigeria have not gained much popularity. There is a Nigeria taste in building and architecture. This is what everyone dreams of building and it is an unwritten code.

Any attempt to use mud, burnt bricks, mixture of cement and earth a gives different aesthetic result and most people have not fully embrace it.

These unconventional building methods are popular in east Africa, India and China. They have mastered the use of various sizes of mud bricks using very little cement content in these countries. Some simply assembly the bricks in an interlocking form (saving cost of mortar) and even where structures are necessary they employ few iron rods. The degree of cost cutting achievable will vary but it said to be substantial. The only problem is that not enough people have tried it and told others. So it remains relatively unpopular.

If you are intent on saving cost this way is possible. It is a matter of choice but remains largely experimental because you would not find too many people around to share their experience or teach you how. Many private companies in Nigeria have made spirited attempts to make these relatively new methods popular here. They are always received cautiously in this nation – hardly embraced. The internet has a lot of information on these alternative methods for those who are interested.

How To Beat Inflation

Building a house will take longer if inflation keeps pushing prices up. There is always the threat of paying more for your building over the month or years. Prices of goods and services tend to rise here at the slightest aggravation. If there is a fuel price hike it result in a general wave of rising prices for consumer goods and labour cost. If there is some scarcity, even when temporary, most wholesalers and retailers tend to take full advantage of the occasion to increase price.

The cost of building materials is constantly increasing due to inflation and this distort many individual projections on how much their building will cost. No doubt this factor is responsible for many abandon projects left to rot underneath overgrown bushes in several neighbourhoods because the owners just cannot continue. In fact it is the reason why some have not started at all since every time they save some money to start based on the last quote for the foundation, prices have shifted forward again.

There must be a way round the challenge posed by inflation and there are a few steps to take to mitigate the full effects of inflation and carry on building.

- **Firstly Inflation Will Occur**

Admit that first and foremost. From experience, Nigeria is one of the quickest to adjust price in the world. Once something triggers it, prices just spiral uncontrollably. This is encouraged by weak price control, buoyed by poor budget execution by government and other macroeconomic malfunctions. The issue is how to tamed inflation to allow you to build your own house, most of which are the under listed practical approaches.

Solutions actually started for you the moment you can convincingly pin-point a regular stream of income to apply to your house project. This means you will always have some money to spend to spend for building as you where guided earlier. The only challenge is that the materials and labour the same amount can cover today may reduce sharply when costs rise due to inflation.

Unfortunately, this experience has demobilised so many and work stopped. The way forward is not to stop but stretch things a little bit by achieving every task by stages despite inflation.

Unfortunately, this experience has demobilished so many people in the past and work stopped. The way forward is not to stop but stretch things in a little bit by achieving every task by staging despite inflation.

- **Commit What You Have (Money) To Each Stage: One Stage At A Time**

This is again another upside for those using the on-site method to build incrementally (stage-by-stage). Not only do

> *Tomorrow is a variable that you may not be able to control or predict but maximise today. This means if you have money saved up and all it can do is the foundation, start it off and finish it. If it is the wall or the upper floor decking that is the stage you are and that is all the money you have presently for building – fine, use it up!*

you achieve the whole by taking up each stage, you also achieve the stage at today's price! Tomorrow is a variable that you may not be able to control or predict but maximise today. This means if you have money saved up and all it can do is the foundation, start it off and finish it. If it is the wall or the upper floor decking that is the stage you are and that is all the money you have presently for building – fine, use it up! Even if your savings is a little short and would not complete that stage, stretch a little more to see it through and finish that stage- it is done- then you can pick on the next!.

Let us say the bill you received for foundation cost is N400, 000 and you have this set aside as you start. About the end of foundation building when the concrete cap is being done, it becomes obvious that the workers need N48, 000 more to complete the entire floor which is two-thirds done already. The suggestion is for you to look for that small balance so that you can put paid to that stage. It is tidy and done. Somehow, see every stage as a season of prices. By the time you are ready again perhaps it is the walls now to be raised up, you meet that certain cost would have gone up again depending on the time lapse in-between. Then deal with it at that level and go as far as your money can take you in that stage you have picked on.

Somehow, see every stage as a season of prices. By the time you are ready again perhaps it is the walls now to be raised up, you meet that certain cost would have gone up again depending on the time lapse in-between. Then deal with it at that level and go as far as your money can take you in that stage you have picked on.

In formal building contracting, this process of price adjustment is referred to as variations. The contractor may submit interim certificates and claim variations when prices of items change from the original estimates.

Having understood all these and the simple approach to handling building and pricing, it is paramount that you know the factors that trigger the price increases in Nigeria and how to deftly manouvre to advantage as they occur.

There are two broad types of price increases of building materials:

1. **Factory prices have gone up or the importers have jerked price up by a certain percentage.**

   Local companies like Nigerite Plc, wapco Cement, Tower Aluminum and say Nigerian wire and cable periodically increase price when production costs go up importation cost and customs duty may also rise or foreign exchange goes up to cause importers to cost more.

2. **Some price increases appear seasonal.**

A good grasp of this pattern will surely help some to cut down on building cost and beat inflation. In the rainy season, demand for cement drops because the rains disturb building work. As a result of lower demand, prices also drop as distributors are prepared to take less profit to push out their supply. The opposite is experienced with roofing timber. In the rainy season prices shoot up because loggers are unable to move inside the forest to fell trees enough for the sawmillers. This results in supply shortages and demand is not met. Prices therefore go up, only to reduce as the dry season comes. You can simply anticipate these things and buy your building materials at the right time or season.

Other seasonal price distortions may occur if there is a labour strike in a key industry like cement factories or production is cut because machinery is bad. Even local events may affect local price like the recent Tsunami in Asia was reported to have affected bulk cement imports resulting in over fifty percent price hikes.

For you who is building your own house, what is needful Is your proper interpretation of the cause and effect. This you can achieve by watching events and news both locally and abroad. In these seasonal price differences all it takes is some waiting game. Once machines are repaired or labour resumes work, prices return to normal, then you can buy at normal prices.

Unfortunately if you rush or panic you can pay more. Also if you get the root cause wrong you may wait in vain. That is to say if you mistake a price increase from factory as a result of higher production cost for a seasonal change, your wait can be more costly for a seasonal change, your wait can be more costly. It is therefore useful to be able to investigate and know what is happening for sure.

Grow Your Money!

The very prospect of growing money may sound comical or incredulous to many. Is money now a plant of some sort that

For someone who is struggling to build a house but constantly finds his modest savings is not getting anywhere, one of the best options is to take the seed money her has saved up and grow it. The intention is to increase the money so that it can successfully be used to build.

it should grow?. Apart from the rustling of crisp new notes, there is no hint of any life in money. In spite of the famous chant of a Nigerian praise singer and his request! "Take me to the back of your house where money grows on trees", there is nothing obvious about growing money.

Welcome back to reality. For someone who is struggling to build a house but constantly finds his modest savings is not getting anywhere, one of the best options is to take the seed money her has saved up and grow it. The intention is to increase the money so that it can successfully be used to build. Want to complete your house? Have enough money!

Growing money simply means you should invest it1 a simple investment plan will yield returns/ profit and increase the original sum invested by a percentage. The increase can be very substantial and help your building move forward a great deal. What more? It cuts the time you spend building in half. In a matter of months, your new house can be ready if you successfully grow funds.

Growing money simply means you should invest it1 a simple investment plan will yield returns/ profit and increase the original sum invested by a percentage. The increase can be very substantial and help your building move forward a great deal. What more? It cuts the time you spend building in half. In a matter of months, your new house can be ready if you successfully grow funds.

Someone is already saying if wishes were horses, beggars would ride" If investing money was so easy, everyone would be rich. Unfortunately, investing money carries some risk and while trading with money you can record losses. This is the most common reason why average people prefer to keep their money in the bank and just earn interest instead of toying with the idea of growing it. Well, there is good news. If you want to grow your money for the purpose of using it to build restrict your investment to either the **stock market** or the **property market**. These are two markets that promise the highest return as you take your money are fairly idle forms of investment requiring little work or activity on your part. Also, the upside is often greater experienced than the downside. It is possible to lose money in the stock market and real estate markets but with a little education, the risk is very low compared to the profit yield, unlike many other forms of investment.

This strategy is just perfect for average struggling professional who is barely saving something for his house project than the downside. It is also good for the business owner operating in the informal sector and saving small sums. Suddenly little sums consistently begin to increase and you keep it growing strictly for use in your new building effort. It is equally very good for the salary earner who earns money from one source and is ever struggling to keep up with low savings. Harness this to advantage and very soon you could be building with sums of money much higher than you ever dreamed possible.

GROWING MONEY THROUGH REAL ESTATE

Before the introduction of more sophisticated instruments of investment in real estate such as unit trusts, investment certificates, joint ownership and others, landed property has for centuries, the world over, been a reliable way to wealth. It is best to approach this portion from this simple angle because with a little bit of technicality and detail most people are confused and lost.

Presently in Nigeria, we as a nation are on the verge of such private sector driven investment initiatives in real estate. But before now, ask the average landlord who has two to three housed and maybe a couple of plots which he bought in a layout and he will give you some simple but enduring investment tips. It has a lot to do with real estate investment habits

Most of such folks, old and young understand that with time, year in year out, the value of land and housed keeps increasing. It is a normal, expected occurrence. The way some discovered was to actually buy a plot at a cheap price, maybe with intention of building later.

Then the area developed but the person did not have money to build. Somehow other people interested in building in the now beautiful area begin to offer juicy sums to buy over such plots that have become prime land. Suddenly, what looked like a small cost has become a source of substantial earnings.

Upon such discovery, most smart people just continue to seek opportunity to buy, sell and build until they have they have a vast estate. Let us be real, this is the story of most people who bought cheap in Surulere, Ikeja, Victoria Island and even more recently Lekki axis in Lagos. Better still, those who move with IBB to Abuja, Federal Capital City in 1992 and bought plots in Maitama and Wuse for 200,000 at that time will confirm the pleasure of their discovery. The early resellers let go at price between 10 to 15 million naira in the late nineties but now such plots go for as high as 45 million naira or more depending on where they are situated. Now consider the huge difference between cost and how much the plots finally sold for? Wouldn't you agree that the money has grown?

The average worker, who is unable to save up a lot of money at any one time, may want to give up on growing money in an appreciable way. It just appears impossible to achieve. But if you look at the simple fact that every town or city has its prime areas where land cost a lot and outskirt where land cost less, you would agree that there is hope for everybody. The further out you are from the town centre, the cheaper it is to afford. The less the infrastructure like electricity, roads, water and telephone, the less cost per plot.

As long as your savings are a bit reasonable you should be able to get a plot to buy. A good starting point for a determine person is find out what it cost to buy such cheap plots and save towards it. This is the minimum possible point of entry.

In Module 2, the idea of buying one plot of land every year was introduced. Anybody who can successfully do this for six years would automatically have a minimum of four to six plots. The challenge of how to secure the plots from trespassers will be fully examined in the next module but it is useful to note that the market worth of those plots put together six years later will almost finish the construction of a whole house. Now it does not have to take six years – it can be much shorter.

Some people have developed the skill of handling investments such that they always buy at the right time and place. You never sell at the price you bought since prices always move up. It is therefore expected that you will reap multiple of what you put in. what more – the area or neighbourhoods that were not okay before for building houses begins to open up.

Infrastructure such as electricity and access roads encourage people to come to new areas (even if the roads are untarred but motorable). The more people are attracted to come, the more they are willing to offer anew to buy plots and prices begin to go up. Such benefit accrues who has since bought when there were no facilities and your asking price goes up. If you do this deliberately and in an organize manner, you could grow your money to substantial levels that can build your own house if you monetize the plots!

Ten years ago (1995), a young broached this idea and acted on it by going ahead to buy first in a medium density estate in Lagos. Fortunately at the time, the real estate boom was not as loud as today. Successively with each fee he earned from professional services, he bought a good residential plot. It took him some discipline because he only spends on basic necessities and was rather frugal. Three years later, he had five good residential plots each securely fenced. In a practical approach as is being highlighted here, he sold four of the plots and retained one to build his house. In one fell swoop, he sold all four plots and cashed the money.

He then proceeded to start a cute 4-bedroom house at Magodo Phase 2 and complete the house within eight months. His earnings at the time really could not build the house but for his smart moves at growing money. And he certainly could not hope to complete a house in one year except for this near miracle of a lump sum he earned by selling off his clever investment of many years.

The above is a true story and the only benefit this young man had was being able to pay for plots periodically straight out of pay cheques which he received for professional services rendered. But why can't other people do the same?

There are workers well paid enough that can buy sizeable well located plots from their savings on monthly salary every three months! The least a worker or small trader can therefore do to achieve this is to cave for twelve months and buy whatever the money can pay in yet another developing part of town

GROWING MONEY THROUGH THE STOCK EXCHANGE

Like real estate, stock and shares can also make your money grow rapidly. Generally speaking, there are investors who

It is realistic to trade shares for a period of time with savings meant for your housing need so that it becomes a more sizeable sum to use in building.

have made all their wealth only through the stock market. Warren Buffet one of the world's richest men made his fortune from stock. The intent here however, is to use the stock market as a medium of growing your savings to help build your new home. It is realistic to trade shares for a period of time with savings meant for your housing need so that it becomes a more sizeable sum to use in building.

One of the beautiful things about the stock market is that it can accommodate smaller sums to buy small units of shares in the company of your choice. If a man can save N10, 000 monthly, he would have to wait till the end of one year to save up to N120, 000 to pay for an average low cost plot of land. The same man can buy shares worth N10, 000 monthly and begin to grow money through this investment channel. It is these small consistent sums when untouched for personal use that will grow substantially over a period of time. This may seem more attractive for people who save sporadically because they achieve their goal without adopting any rigid format.

Think realistically. If you can save up fairly small sums between N10, 000- N20, 000 monthly for 48 months believe it or not you can exit the stock market, cash your money and build your house in a matter of months.

Most people hardly understand the money multiplication principle in the stock market and how it works. There are people who buy shares, oddly enough and yet fail to take full advantage of the remarkable benefits of the stock market. While it may not apply at elementary levels of stock market investments as experience grows you can trade stock actively year in year out instead of just holding on for a long periods, only for capital appreciation.

Three Benefits of Investing in Stock and Shares that accrue to Your Funds

In the stock market you………

i. **Take capital appreciation**/Shares appreciate in unit value over time. The time involved to see appreciable increase may just weeks, months or years. It shall depend on which company's shares you bought the timing and their performance. On the average however, if you buy stock in good companies, often termed blue chips, you can expect the market value of the shares traded on the floor of the stock exchange to go up. If you bought Cadbury Plc for instance a few years back N22 per unit your capital gain presently would be about N28 per unit because each unit of Cadbury Plc's chares is now value at N50 and this can move or slightly dawn at anytime but there is a clear increase per share.

This is the first benefit.

ii.   **Take Dividends.** At the same time that share price is increasing you would be paid dividends after each operational year. Dividends are your own share of profits from the company's annual profits expressed by the number of shares you own. If Guaranty trust bank Plc pays 70kobo per share as dividends you will be paid 70, 000 naira (less withholding tax) if you hold 100, 000 shares of the bank. When shareholding is substantial, dividends can run into millions or hundreds of thousands (naira). This is the second benefit and cannot be overlooked because all three benefits add up.

iii.   **Take Bonus Shares.** The last benefit comes in form of scrip issues or bonus. Based on good performance, high profits and retained earnings of companies, it is usual for the company's management and directors to recommend that each share holder be given a bonus. Bonus share issues are given in addition to whatever you had before as share holder of the company and the share rank equal to each existing share you had.

     In 2004 Nigerian Breweries Plc issues a bonus of one share for every one held by a share holder. If you had 10,000 share, you now have 20,000 shares going for the same price – no differentiation. Of course share price per unit drops almost immediately to reflect this bonus issue but it is a Matter of time. It rises again and share holders reap the benefit by selling at current market price on the floor of the Stock Exchange.

With these three benefits, some people are able to reap more than 100% benefits above their initial investment. Some reap less depending on the dexterity with which stock is handled. The logic of the capital market in which stocks and shares are bought and traded is best understood and handled by a qualified stock broker. Inevitably, it is good to find a stock broking firm registered with the Nigerian Stock

Exchange and get some education from them. Similarly, learn to interpret the result of daily trading on the floor of the Stock Exchange as published in almost all Nigerian daily newspaper. It will help you get a hang of happenings in the stock market.

Armed with more information, every intending house builder can use this approach to swell their funds instead of just straight savings in an idle bank account. This is the way to keep your money working for you without being idle. Yet you are hardly involved since the company into which you bought is doing the actual work. You are merely watching that their performance goes with your expectation otherwise you sell the shares and move on to a better one. Do not loose sight of your goal- as soon as you have converted your savings to enough shareholding that can build, start selling in tranches and apply to building.

There is no harm in continuing with investments in stocks and shares once your building is through and completed since it is proven source of wealth.

CAPITAL MARKET VS PROPERTY MARKET: THE ONLY TRUE MARKETS

Looking for true wealth? You will find it in either of these two markets. A great number of people make mistakes in the past by pitching their tents in the money market. Most preferred this by earning interest on fixed deposits especially because interest rates were astronomical. Ten or fifteen years later, the capital market and property market have emerged stronger while those who entered these two markets early are smiling to the bank today.

The Stock Market Advantages.

- The major advantage of holding shares is the relative ease with which it can be sold off. With a CSCS account (Central Security Clearing System) it takes just about three days to start and finish a sale transaction on the exchange. A house or plot of land will however take months to market or sell depending on the availability of ready buyers.

- Another advantage to shares is that small sums are available to buy some stock you save in bits. Individual holding can therefore increase gradually through micro savings. You need substantial sum to buy landed property. Even bare sites cost lots of money.

- Thirdly, the value of shares is not dependent on the national economy. A Uniliver Plc shareholder living in Lagos cannot get more in returns than a similar share holder living in Ilorin, Kwara State if they sold at the same time. Whereas the equal sum of investment in property would not yield the same result because it depends on local values. Lagos will easily do better in property values than Ilorin. Share performance transcends boundaries of towns and cities but property market result depends on where it located which can turn out to be poor.

The Property Market Advantages

Both markets outperform each other. Sometimes the property market gives better yield, at other times certain selected stock gives abnormally high profit. A lot also depends on the mood of the economy, macroeconomic policy, and individual skill (sheer luck!).

- Property forms a hedge against inflation (see the book *How to Make Huge Profit in Estate Agency*) and as a result will tend to grow in worth every passing year. It is more steady than share price that can dip for a variety of reasons beyond share holders control. A little problem with product quality or poor judgment on the part of the company's management can cause share price to drop. Poor sector performance san cause share price to crash. Such adverse performance can be the result of government policy and suddenly the share are worthless than the prices you initially paid your broker. (The word of advice is to listen to your broker's advice because it is based on information available at each instance – it may be wise to sell and take the loss or hold the stock for some time until price rebounds).

- Property is tangible because it is physically present, unlike share held in certificates and CSCS statements. There is duality about how this works. You can view you property before you always, whether it is a plot of land or a developed property but your share needs a lot of monitoring and control through CSCS (Central Security Clearing System), companies registrars and your broker's care to avoid fraud. The other way however is that activities of fraudsters have also increased in the property market. Plots take more effort to secure and many houses carry the embarrassing inscription "This house is not for sale - beware of 419".

Everyone must ultimately choose where to belong and increase savings and investment. It is advisable to mingle the two markets. Initially, smaller sums may go into the purchase of shares while larger sums are invested in the property market. In each individual case, the focus must clearly lead forward to being able to expend the money gained on building your own property.

ACTION PLAN

1. **Cost cutting**- Again, locate market for following,

Concrete Blocks	Timber	Cement etc
6 inch and 9 inch	Various sizes	

- What are the difference per item?
- Check the distance from your building site and transport cost implications
- Is it still worth the savings you are making?
- If transporting the building materials to your site is too expensive, the price difference between two supply locations may become insignificant.

2. **Cost Efficiency.** Armed with a few tips from what you have read so far, look for a civil/ structural engineer and informally engage in a purposeful discussion about cost saving in design. It will educate you better and prepare you further as you build.

3. **Collect quotes on each stage of building ahead of time.** The foundation walling and lintels, iron rod etc. Are you scared?

This exercise will confront you with a picture of actual sums you may roughly part with at each stage (a bill of quantities will show the same). Whatever your "feelings" you should get it and decide which approach you will need, to start building.

Note- The purpose of this action is to familiarize yourself with costs. It may actually have changed at the time you are finally starting. Cross check prices with whatever is reflected in the bill of quantities.

4. **Set out a time-table months/years to build.** This is should be based on more realistic projections you have now acquired by studying the subject. It may differ from the time projection you wishfully set in the game (give yourself a quit notice under introduction). Having observed adjustments required, you can now realistically build.

5. Take out today's newspaper
    Open the column on the daily capital market report and study the column. You would observe the following

- **It is easy to understand** and once you can interpret this, you can follow developments in the stock market.

- **Sector** Indicates which industry whether banking, insurance or building materials.

- **Company Name** Under the sector are various company names of those publicly quoted with the Nigerian Stock exchange. These are the companies where each of us can buy shares as members of the public

- **Number of deals** Refer to how many transactions that occurred on the floor of the stock exchange that day for that particular company name.

- **Quotation (Naira)-** This is simply the current unit price of each share of the company name under reference. So if you wanted to buy on the floor of the exchange that day that is what it would cost.

- **Quantity Traded-** This is the total number of shares for that company bought and sold that day. This is the addition of shares traded in the number of deals.

- **Lastly the value of shares (Naira)** is the total quantity traded multiplied by the quotation

(Naira). Every day the prices of shares in trading could either go up (gainer) or drop (loser) in trading depends on the forces of demand and supply. This is what you the investor who is trying to grow your money should look out for. It is what helps your own decision as to whether you should buy or sell. For more information and advice visit a qualified stock broker.

- **See Top Gainers**

This is a summary of 5-6 companies and how much they gained on that day of trading.

- **See Top Losers**

A summary of 5-6 companies who lost money on the trading floor and how was lost.

MODULE FIVE

The Cooperative Idea

Cooperatives can be used to achieve a lot in housing people. The challenges that present themselves within the system as almost insurmountable, when individuals make moves to build, are easier to cope with if approached from the angle of using cooperatives. Many people have started realizing this and several Cooperatives and thrift societies have begun all sorts of initiatives for members. This trend has change in recent years, going beyond just the regular savings function for which are popularly known.

The advantage of treating cooperative as a major point in this book is to present the obvious, in an organized manner so that many groups can simply plug into the knowledge and ideas while new forms of cooperative may spring up. The problem with of existing cooperative toying with all sorts of Ideas and concept do far is that there is no real organised approach that can propel the culture of using cooperatives as an active tool to achieve home ownership. Everything relating to cooperative housing presently is jumble and a mixture of everybody's idea, some bold, yet others are timid.

While some may seem to have worked, they can do better and evolve greater focus. Several others have attempted and failed in the past. These can be revived for the benefit of the same members who tried before. The reason for failure or limited success may be attributed to adopting faulty strategy and perhaps then wrong methodology, to using the cooperative concept for housing. Or maybe it is just an idea whose time has come. Whichever way it is viewed, cooperatives can become a hansom tool to helping individuals build their own house in a matter of months. Something that would remain a dream if they did not have the benefit of coming together with others.

The Cooperative Culture

Cooperatives involve people, and if drive, motivation and commitment are lacking, it just would not work. Not because the objectives you want achieve is not clear but because the common passion to build up your contributions *together* is lacking. There must be a common will to keep the cooperative going and functioning. Now this is where the strength of many existing cooperatives lie. A lot of them have evolved systems, bound by a constitution or rules and regulations and they work! If a survey is done across the nation there could be starling discoveries of new science of cooperatives because millions of Nigerians belong to cooperatives, with which they meet their everyday financial challenges!

This is the exact point where the problem can be solved. A quick re-orientation of the focus of each cooperative to help achieve housing needful, while retraining the system and structure that makes the cooperative work in the first instance. Initially people just need an avenue of forced, compulsory savings. Most of these people belong to both the formal sector where you expect a monthly salary and informal sector where there is no pay day, needed an avenue to meet huge lumpsum expenses. Some required such savings to buy a car, meet school fees expenses or even pay for a plot of land. Now the savings are welcome but the focus of the money is spent upon can change to housing and real estate investment habits.

Cooperative can help meet each individuals need for a personal house and only exist to meet more housing needs for new members but also constitute a property investment channel that will yield profit for all members to share and now spent on daily living. It takes us back to reappraise Module 1 and streamline even our compulsory savings to meet the acquisition of appreciating assets rather than spent on depreciating assets.

The idea of cooperatives is enmeshed in our culture which is why we have *"ajo, esusu"* and more – God knows how many ethnic groups have their own version. It is therefore easily welcome who recognize their individual limitations with savings and it can work wonders with housing if used maximally.

The simplest form of cooperatives had few members. For example, (12) people come together and agree to contribute an equal sum monthly. One of the twelve, in turn, simply took home everybody's contributions each month. The other was derived by casting lots and successively a different person took home the joint contributions one after the other each month until the twelve month. Then the whole system revolved again the next year. Of course this approach was fraught with problems such as people dropping off in-between, therefore destabilising projections. Or some who took earnings early refuse latter to keep up their savings having taken money out and deny others of the same benefit.

Today cooperatives are more sophisticated, with greater membership and rules better taught out. Some will lend you a percentage limit above your base savings. In other words, save N200,000 over a minimum period of six months, for example, and you become eligible to borrow three times that amount which is N600,000. Collateral is more simplified when compared to what the banks require. It is based on introducers, social interaction and openness and involvement of the cooperative in what the borrower intends to do with the money.

It all sound very interesting and will get better and more grounded with time. It is a respond to a hard third

> *Eventually even when loans become accessible and mortgage are easy, these cooperatives are unlikely to die because members remain relatively dept free within the cooperative as long as they abide by their compulsory saving habits*

world economic system where loans were almost impossible

to obtain by most people. The conditions were simply too difficult and people found an escape in coming together to form cooperatives. Eventually even when loans become accessible and mortgage are easy, these cooperatives are unlikely to die because members remain relatively dept free within the cooperative as long as they abide by their compulsory saving habits. Your acquisition therefore is almost paid for easily with your savings as compared to outright borrowing from banks.

THREE THINGS TO FOCUS

The cooperative concept can therefore be applied to the following in a focus manner. This is new and inventive. It will tend to allow many more people benefit potentially to achieve their home ownership by joining or forming a cooperative. It can have a sort of mass appeal.

Cooperatives are:

1. **Good for acquiring land.** One of the latent strength of a cooperative is the potential to leverage by purchasing large tracts of land for common hold of members. Your cooperative can achieve the leverage offered only by developers and land speculators

because they buy large acreages and later sub-divide into plots. Now the same is being done by your group and primarily to satisfy the needs of members who want a site to build upon.

2. **Good for buying bulk building materials.** A necessary further step that cooperatives are taking to make building possible for their members. Due to the size of membership and possible bank guarantees that the cooperatives can obtain through the bank, builders' merchants and manufacturers of building materials may open credit lines and give out substantial materials on credit. Members in turn use these in building and pay back through the continuous pattern of savings they are used to. A cooperative may also have a big block making outfit that supplies building blocks to members.

3. **Good for borrowing money to build.** Depending on the objectives of forming a cooperative, the body may loan substantial sums to members for the purpose of building. This is not out of place for many cooperatives who have satisfied the initial yearning of

its members for things like cars and other basic necessities.

> *Imagine a cooperative you join that will sell your plot to you – arrange your supply of building materials direct from manufacturers or distributors on a pay instalmentally- basis and best of all, advance you money to build.*

Certainly, this ought to get many people giving the cooperative idea a good thought. Imagine a cooperative you join that will sell your plot to you – arrange your supply of building materials direct from manufacturers or distributors on a pay instalmentally- basis and best of all, advance you money to build. Some cooperatives already exist that do one part or the other of the above but it appears there is no wholesale approach yet.

FORM OR JOIN COOPERATIVES ALONG THE LINES OF YOUR RELATIONSHIPS.

Birds of the same feather flock together, they say. The easiest way to act upon the bright ideas that come to mind is to take full advantage of the possibilities presented for building houses through cooperatives. And look around you, most people may never have considered the extent of leverage cooperatives can offer, whether or not they belong as members to existing cooperatives. Just knowing it now is also not as useful as acting on the information you now have in order to begin something positive.

Consider forming cooperatives along the following lines:

- <u>The church / mosque cooperative</u>
- <u>The work place cooperative</u>
- <u>The market cooperative</u>
- <u>The professionals cooperative</u>
- <u>The guild's cooperative</u>
- <u>The artisan's cooperative</u>

To which of these do you belong?

Your choice of where to belong or initiate a cooperative will be influenced by the persuasion of those around you and maybe how eagerly they see the prospects and future. Of course beyond the first hurdle of looking for like minds who accept your idea and are ready to birth it with you, there is a greater need for other considerations.

Can you co-habit with your work colleagues because you may end up building together? Will you still be in the same church setting fifteen to twenty years from now?

Are you the sort of person requiring some privacy from your club mates? If you live together, will they pry into your private life?

These are details each person should consciously consider as you fuse and group. From a strictly investment point of view, these are not enough to stop you being a part of such lofty ideas but when you intend to live there, you must satisfy yourself that the parameters are right.

Synergize!! – Let Us Come Together

One of the sore points about raising finance for building and actually doing successfully, for some people, is the individualistic approach. This book has so far enlightened on the huge potency of self help to actualize your own property. By now, many has been helped and should well be on the sure path to home ownership.

There are however many more who do not possess the drive to get up and go! The neither have the sense of organizing needed to put things together. Such people know themselves – they can even successfully arrange their wardrobe. If you are the sort of person who is forever feeling vulnerable when alone and need to have people around you, it is an indication that you are people dependent and cherish the support of others in whatever you do. But don't we all?

The excellent way out of your inaction is to come together with others, usually a small committed group of people and take up the challenge. The common drive of a group can force you along and take over your own lack of drive.

There are some obvious benefits of synergizing, where building your own house is concerned, as highlighted bellow. Remember, at the end of the day it still going to be your own house – what you put in it is what you get. Take out and enjoy all the benefits of synergy but don't cut your own burden on others to carry for you; they may leave behind and finish their own houses.

- **In synergizing, like minds come together**
  Inadvertently, when you are looking for people to join forces with in cooperative housing you will pick on those around you. Those who are your friends, work mates, professional colleagues, acquaintances and relations, they are likely to be your peers, in the same station of life with you. It helps a great deal because

you communicate better and appreciate similar ideals and standards.

- **You chare the risk of land holding**

Quite a lot of people have had bad experiences with land. This range from cases of outright fraud where you paid for land and ended up with nothing, to situations of family land (*omo-onile*) where you paid two or three times consecutively for same plot after terrible harassment. Even where you have not experienced it, you probably have heard enough stories to stop you in your tracks.

This is the reason why many people refuse to take steps to acquire land – the fear of losing it to other claimant since others "owners" may spring up after you pay. Truly, buying bare sites can be hazardous (refer to the book, *How to buy Property Safely in Nigeria* for tips on land buying strategy).

However, when cooperatives buy huge land mass of several acres, it is likely to have involved whole communities or villages. Wide consultations involving family heads, traditional chiefs and rulers and executive members of the cooperative bodies, their agents and solicitors would have taken place.

In such situations where the land is then subdivided for members' ownership, frivolous problems and harassment are less likely. Members are therefore automatically shielded from a lot of potential troubles. This a clear benefit of synergy. If there is ever a problem on such land, it will touch everybody involved and collectively the problem can be tackled.

For instance if the cooperative purchased sixty acres of land and subdivided it into two hundred plots, a fundamental legal flaw like dealing with three family groups instead of five can make the land contract voidable, when eventually the other two groups left out become aware and rise up. In such instances, the problem is legitimate and it is everybody's concern. The risk of land holding is shared. It is more difficult to extort money from two hundred people than individual land owners.

- **You open new areas together**

If you leave in a major town or city for some years, you will clearly observe that some parts are regarded as exclusive locations and the rich and successful will tend to gravitate towards such neighbourhoods. The next thing is that everybody wants to belong there too, until there is no more space when compared with a number of people angling to buy plot and build in those choice areas.

A lot of people are forced to the city outskirts; areas just springing up. The slow pace of development and lack of infrastructure tends to discourage the average person and so people do not want to go there. Cooperative however can afford to move people *enmasse* to new areas, build fair level of infrastructure and suddenly fifty, eighty or one hundred new families settle down in their own homes. It all about shared cost and added value which will be viewed later. Even government at local and state levels will listen quicker to a cooperative group.

- **In synergizing, there is shared security**

  This is today the attraction for gated developments which is becoming a global trend. In South Africa, United Kingdom, United States of America, Spain and Dubai, developers are using the idea of multi apartments secured with gates to sell their new developments. They are perceived as safer.

  The truth is that it is gaining popularity in Nigeria, as a matter of necessity. Even residential neighbourhood that have existed for many decades in Lagos, Ibadan, Port Harcourt without gates have now installed gates to ward off intruders and armed robbers in the night. The problem is made more acute in the outskirts of town where development of houses are far in-between other unbuilt vacant plots. Coming together to develop as cooperatives however makes security a centralized issue and everyone is concerned.

- **Synergy boosts compulsory savings**

  There is such a thing as healthy rivalry. When you see other people with you, targeting a common a goal of home ownership you can be encouraged to do your utmost best. Most ambitious folks will not want their colleagues to leave them behind when they started an idea together meant to promote each other's well being. If before the cooperative effort you spent a lot on personal comfort, it is likely to reduce now because you should concentrate your earnings on keeping up with the pace of development of the others which in turn depends on your savings

- **You have access to a pool of funds**

  This is of great benefit because it increases your cooperative negotiating power for a variety of things. Funds for development are hard to come by and single individual efforts do not often produce a large pool of funds but just by coming together you won't believe the large purse which a lot of people contributing money consistently every month can wield. With such money, you can buy raw land, provide basic infrastructure, lend money to qualified members and carry on massive development together.

In fact, some cooperatives grow large enough to command power like financial institutions and end up operating mortgage based products.

- **Synergy can produce substantial cost benefits.**
  The simple principle of buying in bulk help to save cost significantly. Breaking bulk to distribute to members tends to produce the unit cost each person has to pay and this you achieve by merely coming together. This cost saving can apply to land costs, approval costs, professional fees, building materials cost and a host of other things. This is the power of housing cooperatives in the setting of a developing country.

- **Lastly, you can raise money for self build beyond the immediate.** This benefit is usually more achievable when you join cooperatives that have been on ground for some time. Borrowing is easier after contributing for some months and you can be advance a good sum of money, which would have been much more difficult with individual savings habits.

In a way it works vice versa because your regular savings are now committed towards repayment of the loan. By this time, you would have made huge strides in progress building your house and all you have to worry about is paying your dept at reasonable interest rates. You beat time because you have your home faster and inflation since you have built at today's cost.

Form Your Own Site And Service And Service Scheme

Today's up and coming have their eyes on the good things of life. High flyers want to ride good cars and build their house in Victoria Garden City, Lagos or at least Lekki Phase 1. Where neither of the two is possible, they opt for other locations in Ajah, Osapa London and all the other estates now extending fast towards Epe Township. Anyone would wonder – why the sudden craze and rush for these locations? The answer lies in the appeal these areas have, with great beauty and architectural splendor, build in planned neighborhoods, well laid out and installed with all infrastructures.

This trend in housing development is not limited to Lagos Island but also the mainland of Lagos, then Port Harcourt, Warri and Abuja. A few years back, only the state and the Federal Government have the capacity to build housing estates but in the last decade, private developers have sprung up to create even better estates. It started with Dolphin estate build by HFP Engineering which was very successful. More recently, indigenous companies like Cornerstone Construction Company and a host of others, have created wholly build estates as well as service sites ready for building. The idea of site and services is to provide all necessary facilities around the plots or site, so that all that is required is to build the house and move in.

Service Commonly Provided

- Road network
- Sidewalks
- Electricity
- Telephone facilities
- Boreholes/mains water/pipe network
- Drainage

- Recreational facilities (swimming pool, lawn tennis, squash court, etc.)
- Entrance gate house and communal security.

This pattern of development is likely to continue. Developers are having a field day and smiling to the bank. The plots in their estate or site and service scheme cost several millions and are now even sold per square meter!

A lot more people who cannot afford to pay millions of naira wish to have plots to build their houses in serviced estates and buy plots at lower cost. The good news is that you can cut off the developer's the moment you can form a

A lot more people who cannot afford to pay millions of naira wish to have plots to build their houses in serviced estates and buy plots at lower cost. The good news is that you can cut off the developer's the moment you can form a group of like minds who are ready to create their own estate or site and serviced scheme!

group of like minds who are ready to create their own estate or site and serviced scheme!

In other words, you pay for the plot and services at cost. It suddenly become affordable because for the same sort of environment others paid several millions of naira for, you pay about half price. A good example is the cooperative villa, Lekki, Lagos which was formed several years ago, by group of young professionals. They came together under a cooperative umbrella and bought vast underdeveloped land, cleared it and allocate to members under strict guidance. Today they have created fully built thriving communities and embark on other phases.

So why can't you look around you for people who feel ready to acquire land for a site and serviced scheme and begin to discuss with them?

- **It's easy:** initially your group may be small or large depending on where the idea is being generated and the people involved.

- **Think along the line of your church groups,** workplace, social clubs and other lines of relationships earlier suggested in this Module.

- **Estimate the size of land you will all require:** This can be done by standardizing each plot size on the average. Multiply by the total number of plots anticipated and add some more to allow for a road network and other common areas.

- **Begin the process of land assembly:** This will cause you to repeat some of the steps earlier suggested in this book. The key point is to jointly agree on the direction of city growth. Which areas are promising and coming up fast with new development? Whether you are in Lagos, Enugu, Port Harcourt, Akure, Kano or Jos, these parts of town are fairly easy to analyse and seek out. Acquire what you need by buying several acres from the present owners. The process is not as simple (refer to the book, *How to Buy Property Safely in Nigeria*) and get professional help.

- **Do the layout/subdivisions:** This is where you begin to engage professionals. Remember, in the early stages, you need a land surveyor to establish the boundaries of your land. You now require the services of town planner to carve up or cut the several acres into the plot sizes you need. A qualified town planner will know how to relate the plots to the road network and provide for services such as schools, markets or shopping areas, recreational facilities, etc. The extent of his provision primarily is determined by the size of the project and the number of families that will occupy the anticipated community.

Open spaces, green areas and setbacks are some of the other provisions a professional will make while subdividing.

- **Next is site clearance:** Virgin land may have trees that need to be uprooted and thick bush or forest to cut down, so you will have clear site to build upon. Usually you will need to arrange heavy earth moving equipment, like caterpillars and bulldozers. Again the cost is shared and the use of hired equipment maximized.

  When you clear land, you suddenly appreciate it better. Two hundred acres of cleared vegetation will now look open and exciting. Life seems to come on the site and surface is now prepared for further building preparation.

  The more detail preparation now begins with an intricate effort by a team of building professionals working together to put the details of the master plan designed on paper now on the ground.

Swiftly they mark out each plot with beacons, establish the access road network within the estate. All the professionals involved, ideally should have site meetings, to work out the most efficient way to the preparation of a bare ground ready for building. Some of them can work simultaneously while others wait for one task or the other to be completed before starting theirs. As a result, they can make critical path analysis of all activities and finish up in record time.

- Typically, the road construction can go on as soon as the roads are demarcated, while the land surveyors put beacons on each plot. Once the drainage which acts as borders for the road are in place, the road can be paved or tarred and the side walk can be built.
- If telephone or electric cables are to be buried, it should be agreed what time this can be done so there is symmetry. It no use having to break pavements to install pipes and cables, if it is possible to install them prior to paving surfaces.

  Generally, every step and level must be well thought out before execution.

THE COST FACTOR

Again the cost considerations come into all these lofty ideas. Any group of people coming together to form site and service schemes should try to estimate typical costs. Fairly detail calculations of every cost involved from site acquisition to surveys, professional fees, site clearance, cost of site preparation and installation of infrastructure should be done. It will wrong to assume or guesstimate anything about cost. It may also be wise to make an allowance for contingencies that may arise in the course of development.

Note: consciously understand that your group does NOT have to operate the ideal estate, in site and services. You may all decide just to bulldoze the roads and open up the site for now, while individual plot owners take over the rest of the things, like individual plot survey cost and so on.

Remember, what you put is what you get – the more you can afford in cost the more the more features you can add to make your estate ideal and vice versa. There are layouts that are not fully serviced, only partial – sometimes the early residents are the ones that contribute money together to buy NEPA poles and cables to bring electricity to their own part of the layout or estate – or is it now PHCN? Whatever you do should be a conscious effort.

UNDERSTAND COST IN SITE AND SERVICES PROPERTY

When a lot of people are involved and cost has to be shared on fair and principled bases, it can become confusing. The crude proposition with many cooperatives already involved with land purchase scheme for members is to buy land in acres and simply share the cost per plot. If the cooperative bought 20 acres of land for N24 million and subdivided into 80 plots, the tendency is to divide N24 million by eighty. At best they share survey cost and the cost of hiring a bulldozer for initial clearing equally and leave it at that. Subsequently, it is each member for himself in this intermediate layout. This does usually turn out the best.

The outcome of a site and serviced scheme can be better than this, with good planning from the beginning. This also translates into a better way to define the cost inputs. There are two broad headings of cost in site and services: primary and secondary costs.

- **Primary cost:** As described above, primary cost relate to the cost of site acquisition, the cost of subdividing, or preparing the layout plan, as many understand it. It relates all cost to the point of delivering your plot to you. Things like survey costs of individual plots, bush clearance, etc. This is where a lot of groups end their costing.

- **Secondary costs:** These are also known as off- street cost. They include the cost of providing infrastructure everywhere in the estate. Every cost incurred on the estate as you step out of your own plot into the street comes under secondary costs. Usually there should be a sharing formula of the secondary cost calculated per square metre. So when a developer sells land in a site and service scheme at N4,500 per square metre, both primary and secondary cost have been included.

Another way of working out secondary cost is the linear method. What goes past your frontage is your own to bear. This is to say, just tar your house frontage and buy the time each person bears the cost of storm drainage, walkway and road in front of his house the whole estate is done. Your choice as group depends on how far you want to go with provision of services in your site and service scheme.

JOIN AS MANY COOPERATIVE SCHEMES AS YOU CAN AFFORD

Early in this book, Module 1, the idea of buying a plot each year from your savings was muted. This achieves two things for the individual – first you sharpen your real estate investments habits and learn to invest. Second, its enable you build a reservoir of assets which appreciate quickly and you can sell your plots to utilize the profits in building your own house.

All these are true. The challenge however has always been how keep the plots you buy from trespassers. A greater percentage of folks who bought land in the past suffered losses, unaware of the pitfalls. While it is possible to minimize the risk of being swindled in land transactions (see the book, *How To Buy Property Safely in Nigeria*), it is safer to hide away in cooperative schemes.

You can appreciate this better if you have studied the benefit of synergizing (in this Module) – the risk of land holding is shared! *Omo-onile* (land owning families) cannot just come to your own plot in cooperative schemes. They are likely to approach the whole group and believe it, even for them, it more difficult than messing about with individuals. So for a lot of reasons, it saver to purchase land in cooperative efforts.

To achieve this, you can join several cooperatives and participate in each scheme – join the church/mosque cooperative, join your workmates, join your club mates, etc. Bear in mind the investment principle; you are creating wealth so forget your personal preferences. The attraction is being able to keep these plots, whether or not you can build fence walls. In the years to come, the cooperative concept will become stronger, more acceptable and defiantly more visible.

Action Plan

1. Do already belong to a cooperative society?
    - If yes, is your cooperative involved in acquiring plots for members benefit?
    - Are you planning the cooperative further to make housing possible?
    - If your answers to these questions are in the affirmative then you are right on track.
    - You may want to suggest involving the relevant building professionals to make it better.

2. If you said no, that is that you don't belong to any cooperative body at all, you may consider the following:-

- Ask around your location for existing and reliable cooperatives that are functioning that you can join.
- Find out about the sort of membership they have and the condition of membership.
- Also ask what relevance they have to your housing goals.

3. If your findings so far are unsatisfactory you begin to consider starting a cooperative body with a few others interested in your vision.

- Begin by doing some research into various types of cooperative structures and how they run/operate.
- Compare and contrast in other to evolve a potential system that can work.
- Try calling and initial meeting/discussion group about your idea to see how much support you have.

4. Based on (Point 3) above if you are going ahead to form a cooperative you should call meetings to agree on the *modus operandi.*

   - Draw up a constitution. Agree on rules and regulations.
   - Attempt to define the scope of the cooperative you are about to form.

5. Consider a simple exercise. Understand site and services by visiting existing ones. Some of these can be located via newspapers and advertorials. The essence is to familiarize yourself with services and say standard you, standard you want to attain.

6. Lastly with the aim of benefiting from synergy, plan to visit new areas where you can potentially purchase large tracts of land.

   Remember Module 2 – (study the direction of city growth)? This is the point where you should apply knowledge gained.

MODULE SIX

Take a mortgage!

Nigeria will not always suffer from the economic malaise that causes credit and loans to disappear. Presently individual persons have very limited access to loan from financial institutions. There are many reason why this is so and the prescribe cures are therefore several.

- Banks attract funds from depositors to do their business of lending (current and savings accounts) with a promise to pay interest but cannot keep such

> *Presently individual persons have very limited access to loan from financial institutions. There are many reason why this is so and the prescribe cures are therefore several.*

sums for long period because the depositors usually call for then within relatively short periods (3-12 months). Banks therefore unable to lend for mortgage loans that people will use to build their houses. Such loans require several years to repay ranging from 5 to 25 years.

Hopefully the present Central Bank of Nigeria policy asking banks to recapitalize their capital base to N25 billion should remove this handicap. Having gone through this re-engineering, banks should have money to commit to long term repayment loans. The full effect of this will unfold from year 2006 and beyond.

- Banks wants to safeguard their interests when they lend money out to a borrower. They demand for an asset from a borrower to collaterize the loan, so that they have something to hold un to, in case of default in this environment. The business environment is harsh and causes people's income to dwindle and repayment is difficult. The problem is also compounded by borrower's unethical practices, like marrying more wives and spending on personal luxuries instead of applying loans for what it was approved for. Lastly, situations of outright fraud – borrower just wanted the money and never intended to repay. Lessons learnt over time by financial institutions, have cause them to tighten the noose. Only few people qualify to take loans and can provide the required collateral over. Therefore only few people actually get loan or credit.

As far as housing is concerned, with ongoing banking reforms couple with the new National Housing Policy, mortgage loans can hopefully be granted many more people with the house standing as security. The moment you qualify with a set criterion to build or buy a house, you will be given a mortgage loan but with a proviso. If you default in repayments, your will be repossessed by the lender to recover the loan.

- The National Housing Fund took off in 1991, with the hope of creating a pool of resources for mortgage lenders to assess. The benefit was intended for workers, civil servants and contributors to the fund who should have saved a certain sum for a consistent minimum of six months top qualify.

For years after 1991, people contributed and the NHF grew its funds but it did not translate to mortgage loans when several people should have qualified. Somewhere along the line, either because of lack of commitment on the part of the government or a creaky untested machinery for loan delivery, the mortgage system just could not take off. The Umbrella body, FMBN – Federal Mortgage Bank of Nigeria being the apex and regulating body clearly had a problem. Labour organizations protested to continued deductions from workers salaries – why keep taking money from workers when it is clear that you do not intend to give the money back as building loans?

This is the state of things with the mortgage sector and the reason why mortgage have not been disbursed enmasse through the Primary Mortgage Institution (PMIs) to date.

- Apparently since Nigeria's new democracy began in 1999, it has been the undisguised posture of the

The national housing fund then becomes useful and people can benefit, contributors will be encouraged and continue. The challenge has been how to jump start it to have mass appeal that the common Nigerian can benefit from. Government at both ends wants to stimulate demand and encourage supply!

Olusegun Obasonjo led government. Apparently since Nigeria's new democracy began in 1999, it has been the undisguised posture of the Olusegun

Obasonjo led government not to get directly involved with building houses for people. In the past as government observed, most of these efforts had failed. Government now prefers to encourage private developers to build houses for the people. The reckon that if they can successfully get this going, private developers will build estates of various types, some for low income groups and some for the high and mighty. The buyers in turn can approach mortgage banks to borrow money in other to buy. The national housing fund then becomes useful and people can benefit, contributors will be encouraged and continue. The challenge has been how to jump start it to have mass appeal that the common Nigerian can benefit from. Government at both ends wants to stimulate demand and encourage supply!

This is the nut that Professor Akin Mabogunje led Presidential committee on housing has been cracking for a few years now. Evidently, they have made substantial progress and soon the mortgage machinery will be fully oiled and working. What is the evidence? Through all the preparatory work and the just and may announcements of policy direction only, a lot of private developers have sprung up already. Some of them have been aided by the federal government either to help attract financing for their housing schemes or given substantial land allocation to site their new developments (Public/ Private Participation)

Definitely, when completed, the mortgage process will record a degree of success. Whether it will become as efficient as those of the United Kingdom, South Africa, the USA and other developed nations we cannot tell yet. It will take years for this to take full form and very soon it is anticipated that the average Nigerian take a mortgage to buy or build his own house.

- The institutions that will be involve in financing your mortgage:
- Central Bank of Nigeria
- Federal Mortgage Bank of Nigeria
- Commercial Banks
- Primary Mortgage Institutions (Mortgage Banks)
- Insurance Companies (Pension Funds. Etc.)
- Urban development Banks

- The Nigeria Stock Exchange.

- How will mortgage lenders recover if the mortgagor defaults and is unable to pay back his loan? Before now the Federal Mortgage Bank and other commercial banks in their experience are dragged to court to stop sale of property by owing customers. The legal process is slow and frustrating. This makes it rather cumbersome for the lending institution to recover money in good time. Borrowers took advantage of this in the past to buy time and prolong the time needed for loan recovery. A lot of such loans end up being classified as bad depts. These banks do like this, hence their reluctance to give out long-term mortgage facilities. The law in Nigeria is not brisk to decide on matters of loan discovery and authorities that such houses held as collateral should be sold.

- One the cures being applied now, courtesy of the presidential committee on housing, are changes being proposed for existing laws that will remove clogs to repossession of mortgaged property. When the bills are eventually amended and passed by the national assembly, there will be less red tapism with mortgage arrangements and lenders will be able to recover houses once they can establish that the borrower has defaulted and refused to pay for specified months. If this is not done, the system will have a problem. It will be forced to slow down because a lot of money will be out there, stuck in the houses of people who are not paying. Yet theses housed cannot be sold to recover money for the NHF so that others waiting for loans can benefit. The legal system is crucial to the success of the proposed mortgage system.

Under this scenario, a borrower must be helped to understand the implication of taking a mortgage loan and abide by the conditions. The law must side the mortgage lender to be able to take effective possession of the property and auction it for the sake of the mortgage system.

In the United Kingdom, there is uniform warning on every standard mortgage pack or form- ***"your home is a risk if you do not keep up your mortgage payments"***. If you default on payments for three consecutive months and do not have insurance back up in case of a job loss, or other handicaps, you may be dispossessed of your house.

- High interest charges made it virtually impossible in the last two decades to borrow money for building residential housing. Loans could only be repaid when applied to certain classes of business in the Nigerian economy that yield good profit margins-imports, LPO financing and contracts. A long term mortgage loan is expected to be repaid, either through the savings from the property. The interest rate is therefore usually low, all over the world. A slight increase in interest charges can upset repayment and this is taken into consideration by serious governments everywhere.

- The goals of the ongoing housing reforms seem to be

Under this scenario, a borrower must be helped to understand the implication of taking a mortgage loan and abide by the conditions. The law must side the mortgage lender to be able to take effective possession of the property and auction it for the sake of the mortgage system.

working together with Central Bank of Nigeria's broad banking reforms. Due to recapitalization and mergers to form bigger, stronger commercial banks, interest rates are tumbling down. Base lending rate is down, interbank lending rates are much lower. It is hoped that interest rates will fall to a single digit and remain so. This will make mortgage lending feasible and stable. This is the last ingredient needed in the palliative for the mortgage sector.

In NIGERIA, YOU SHOULD TAKE A MORTGAGE ONLY IF or WHEN all these factors are in place. Things are pointing in the right direction and predictably it is a matter

> *This means you must still cultivate a savings habit to successfully borrow and repay. Not just that, if your outflow is too high, you fall behind in regular repayments, then huge debts accrue. You have lost control-you are no longer in the driver's seat. This is unlike buildings incrementally, when you can choose your pace, style and time. It all remains a matter of choice and economics.*

of "when" not "if". As a result, it is one of the avenues through which housing will be financed by individuals to make it possible to build your own house in a matter of months. It is therefore needful to include it in this book for a clear x-ray or analysis. Remember, if you borrow, you must plan to pay the mortgage loan. Your own personal savings however, when applied to building, leaves you debt free after the exercise. Does it now indicate that mortgage loans are bad? NO-as a matter of fact, you build or buy at today's cost. You therefore beat inflation. But at what cost? What is the cost of funds?. If the interest rate is too high, the borrower ends up paying high rates back to the lender. To amortize the loan, far in excess of the cost of inflation. He then takes heavy losses and may not be able to manage the negative loan outflow from his pocket.

This means you must still cultivate a savings habit to successfully borrow and repay. Not just that, if your outflow is too high, you fall behind in regular repayments, then huge debts accrue. You have lost control-you are no longer in the driver's seat. This is unlike buildings incrementally, when you can choose your pace, style and time. It all remains a matter of choice and economics.

Low cost of funds makes it attractive to use other people's money to build, so take a mortgage and pay back through your savings. But fluctuating, unpredictable or high interest rates are no good. As long as the system is shaky, go it the old fashioned way.

ONCE UPON A TIME

It is good to learn from history. There was a period in Nigeria's history when mortgage were given. There is a careful attempt so far not involved in writing the theory of mortgages or engaging in dates and historical facts or background. Why is this so? The truth is, mortgages are not working in the seamless beautiful way the work in developed countries here. Any attempt to pain picture ends up sounding too academic. Really, what this book should achieve is help you to think right and understand mortgages. If you are taking a mortgage, do so with the right judgment – simple. And make sure you get out it intact, without loosing your house. Then this book would have been worth it.

Many people took mortgage loans from the Federal Mortgage Bank in the seventies. Several houses were built in the south west, south east and northern Nigeria with the aid of these mortgages. Two things began to occur.

1. **The borrowers were rather relaxed about payment of the mortgages.** Many took it at their own pace and paid what they could, whenever. They did not understand the principle of compound interest. Some erroneously thought paying the rent accruing from the building straight to FMBN was the way to service the mortgage.

   Unfortunately, those rents were often lower than even the annual interest charges and got swallowed up in compound interests calculations.

Their outstanding loans balance swelled yearly, beyound what they could understand, yet many remain complacent. In fact, some fleetingly thought it was part of their own chare of the infamous "National Cake".

2. **Years of military and democratic misrule in the seventies and eighties led to escalating interests rates.** These mortgages were not "capped interest rates". The initial rates at which the loans were taken were single digit. They spiral higher and higher to about 23% per annum over a period of many years. The combined effect of this and compounded interest made several mortgage loans impossible to pay back.

Under this old regime, quite a lot of people lost their houses to the auctioneer's gavel. Long drawn battles were engaged in court and after several years of legal hassles, the courts upheld the right of the bank to the sale. These lessons must not be lost on the future when the mortgage system picks up again. A lot of the past beneficiaries through 1970s were educated and enlightened. They however did not have financial intelligence and remained relatively ignorant.

TODAY'S MORTGAGES

Some forms of mortgages are still available in Nigeria today. There are very few genuinely mortgage institutions. This is due to operational difficulties highlighted before in Nigerian business environment for this sector. Some mortgage institutions use the funds available to them to trade in real estate. Some of the active ones remain Union Homes (A subsidiary of Union Bank Plc) among others.

The few mortgage products available to the public therefore were engineered by some of these institutions to suite the present stage of things.

Today's mortgages attract high interest rates still in double digits. Averagely just 2-3% below commercial lending rates. This is still not suitable for the need of most people who wanted to build.

- **Today's mortgages** attract high interest rates still in double digits. Averagely just 2-3% below commercial lending rates. This is still not suitable for the need of most people who want to build.

- **Today's mortgages** are often packaged with the backing of some active, new generation commercial banks who have begun to take an interest financial real estate developments. These banks have realized that in the long term, banks will have little choice but to finance real estate. Presently, the nature of the funds available is inimical to full participation. They therefore carefully package mortgage deals fairly short term; 2 to 10 years at high rate of interest. These are available to targeted income earners or for investment in high brow areas like Ikoyi, Victoria Island, Lagos or Maitama, Asokoro in Abuja where the payback period is short and promising.

- **Today's mortgages** have little bases for policy or broad management guidelines. Rather these mortgages are often designed by financial institutions per use or per project (estate development). In other words, if a development is build in Port Harcourt where the majority of buyers anticipated are oil services workers who can pay substantial sums monthly, the bank may package a mortgage facility for only 18 months of heavy monthly repayments and it suits that peculiar market. New generations banks are most active in providing these facilities and will alter the approach where necessary in another location.

In realty **today's mortgages** are not a walk-in-affair. It is fairly difficult today to raise money of the cuff to build your house through the mortgage banks. Even where it is possible you may be paying a commercial rate of interest. Can you cope?

TOMORROW'S MORTGAGES

From the 2006-2007 and beyond, mortgage banks are expected to take up with batter packaged mortgages, most of which will be home grown and adapted to suite our financial sector. There is a loud rumble as the newly recapitalised are kindly organizing in-house ambitious mortgage banking subsidiaries.

Funds are anticipated for PMI's from three sources:

1. **They can draw from the National Housing Fund:** by this time, the mortgage system should be fully set to operate with all the change being made already in place.

2. **Funds can be made available from the over N25 billion that all banks now possess.** Banks are eager

to play in all viable sectors and the mortgage industry looks promising to them, hence the present on-going preparations.

3. **Funds will flow in from various international sources.**

   Once the mortgage system is in place and the repayment structure grounded, a lot of foreign investors are expected to scramble for a place in Nigeria's housing sector. The burgeoning middle class has an unbelievable number of potential buyers running into millions of households. These are the middle class who can afford to payback gradually which is all that is required to sustain a robust mortgage system.

For the first time in a long time, the average income or salary earner will be able to take a mortgage. Various mortgage plans will be unfolded by the Primary Mortgage Institutions (PMIs), who are the retailers of mortgage products by design. An atmosphere of competition is likely to be generated, as such banks tries to attract new customers to take a mortgage loan either to build or to buy.

The more competitive the Nigeria mortgage sector becomes, the more attractive it will be for the average worker to approach them for a facility. More and more people will therefore qualify. By the time stability is achieved in the financial sector, *ceteris paribus,* banks should be willing to fund longer term mortgages at lower interest rates and still appreciate the sort of profit returns they will make. How long the term of the loan will be and what interest rates will be market determined over time. It will turn out to be similar to the experience of the telecoms industry. When the GSM service providers obtained their licenses and first rolled out, calls were charge per minute (not "per seconds") and each minute cost N50 and if you talk for one minute two seconds you still pay paid N100 charge as two minutes!

Today competition has tamed price and there are a variety of packages with cost costing as low as N10-18. This trend will also occur in the mortgage sector and evolve with good mortgages overtime to the advantage of the borrower in the mortgage industry.

The above is critically based on predictions of a stable Nigeria, both politically, all things being equal. For the individual, it is okay to digest all these for better understanding of mortgages and watch it all unfold. As soon as you observe that everything is on track you can then exercise your power of choice. You are now the bride that the mortgage banks are trying to court.

There are three angles from which to judge better mortgage offers as they come to you through the national dailies, billboards and their marketing staff.

1. **Mortgage Duration:** What is the extent of time you are being allowed to repay gradually. The longer the period the better to enable you, the borrower, spread your monthly repayments for convenience. Obviously from the short term culture, they are coming from; offers of 25years may come with stiffer conditions. The more convenient offers may be for shorter ranges. Look out for this.

2. **Interest rate:** The rate of interest payable on a mortgage loan or any borrowing whatsoever

> *The rate of interest payable on a mortgage loan or any borrowing whatsoever translates to cost for the borrower. That cost is always something to watch or else your income may not be able to support scheduled repayments.*

translates to cost for the borrower. That cost is always

something to watch or else your income may not be able to support scheduled repayments. Due to competition, mortgage banks will play on rates-some may offer 9% or 9.5% or 11% depending on their strength or strategy (the above are used for illustration only. Rates will be determined by the market and apex regulatory bodies-Central Bank of Nigeria/Federal Mortgage Bank of Nigeria). The borrower can then make a choice.

3. **Flexibility:** Mortgage lenders are in banking to make money. Their profit comes from the interest charges you pay on capital borrowed. The longer such cash flows subsist, the better for profit and long – term planning. Their balance sheet will look very good with regular cash inflows coming in from so many borrowers. Some mortgage banks therefore set stiff obstacles for people who just want to use mortgage funds quickly and get out for early repayments. For instance, someone may want to pay back within three years even though the initial mortgage contract duration was fifteen years, if he suddenly makes a windfall in business. Some mortgage institutions may not want this at all-the longer the merrier.

Competition will however force all sorts of flexible packages and the individual borrower can exercise some choice.

As you consider taking a mortgage, you must look out for the possibility of an early redemption as well as other flexible features in the mortgage you are taking. All these are the picture of future mortgages in Nigeria. It is good to anticipate these with knowledge and use whatever you learn now at every point, as it becomes relevant.

One Loan, Many Savings

To buttress the way mortgages think, there was a business meeting in 1993 involving one of the surviving mortgage banks, then newly licensed, under the 1991 National Housing Policy. Someone then pronounced their name ending with "Savings and Loans". Their executive director cheerfully retorted "Point of correction! Only on loan but many savings". As much as it sounds like a joke, it underlies the truth. Traditional, an average individual only qualifies to take one mortgage loan in a lifetime and spends the rest of his life servicing it.

Now, in the United Kingdom and United States of America, real estate the legislation has been amended several times over the years and this enables financially smart people to use several mortgages to buy property with little or no deposits. These investors deftly use their leverages and profit earnings to pay back their mortgage over a period of years. This may also be achievable in Nigeria someday when full flexibility is attained. In the mean time be smart enough to make the right choices so that you can be a winner. You are a winner only if you can take that one loan and successfully pay back to redeem your house from the bank's hold. Only then is it wholly yours.

FOR PROFESSIONAL ESTATE SERVICES CONTACT

Marvtech Network Solution

Estate Surveyors & Valuers Developments Appraisers

OUR SERVICES:

ESTATE AGENCY- letting Services,Buying and Selling property within LAGOS,IBADAN,ABUJA, PORTHARCOURT

SPECIALIZATION- sourcing factories,Officesand residence for international companies coming to Nigeria.

VALUATION: We undertake:Valuation of company Assets and valuation for all purposes.

PROPERTY DEVELOPMENT: We x-ray proposed development to increase the chances of success by undertaking feasibility Studies

PROPERTY/FACILITY: MANAGES-Day to day managment of substantia properties and high-rise building.

For MORE ENQUIRY, CALL: +2348077824698 E-mail:marvtechnetworksoluion@gmail.com